AF485242

Praise for

EQUUS FLIGHT ACADEMY

"A wonderful, easy-to-read coming-of-age story I'd recommend to all the young people in my life! This author is one to watch!" —*Amy White, The White Editorial*

"I really loved this world! It has you feel all the feelings–made you feel like you were actually flying a pegasus, falling in love, and growing up. It's giving spice-free Fourth Wing vibes and dragon riding academia vibes. I highly recommend this clean romantasy to all! I was so happy to see a YA book actually be YA." —*J.R*

"I really enjoyed getting to read an advanced copy of this book! It had good pacing to it and a unique storyline. I thought the main character was very relatable and likeable. I would definitely recommend this book if you like a nice clean romance with a fantasy school setting!" —*O.S*

Equus Flight Academy

HANNAH FLUKER

This is a work of fiction. Characters, names, places, and incidents
are either the product of the author's imagination or used fictitiously.
Any resemblance to actual persons, living or dead, businesses, companies, events, or
locales is entirely coincidental.

Copyright © 2026 Hannah Fluker

All rights reserved.

Cover by Hannah Fluker

IBSN (paperback)
979-8–9955643-0-0

No part of this book may be used or reproduced in any form or by any electronic or
mechanical means, including information storage and retrieval systems, without written
permission from the author, except for the use of brief quotations in a book review.
Names: Fluker, Hannah, author.
Title: Equus Flight Academy / Hannah Fluker.
Description: First edition. | Audience: Ages 12 up. | Subjects: YA fantasy fiction.

To all the girls who'd rather fly

a Pegasus…

"But those who trust in the Lord
will renew their strength;
they will soar on wings like eagles;
they will run and not become weary,
they will walk and not faint."

Isaiah 40:31

Chapter 1

Today has to be the day. I grasp the steering wheel tighter and turn into the driveway, wrinkling my nose at the pungent aroma of diner food now permanently infused into my car this summer.

I let out a breath, blowing at the pale strands of hair that fell from my ponytail. It's too easy to rip off my name tag and apron, flinging them to the passenger side. Relief floods me, and a smile spreads across my lips. I grab my purse and step out into the warm breeze.

The one-story yellow house seems smaller today as excitement bubbles up in my chest. I rush down the driveway to the mailbox and fling open the handle. It could be any day now, right? One letter. One single letter could change my life forever.

Here goes nothing…

I swipe the letters from the box and hold them up, running

my fingers over the smooth paper. It better not just be bills. I shriek with excitement when I see it.

"University of Cincinnati."

But it's way too small to be an acceptance letter…

My heart sinks. I take a shaky breath, blinking hard before flipping through to the next one.

"Equus Flight Academy."

What on earth is this? I flip it over and examine the wax seal of a Pegasus in mid-flight. Should I open it?

I flip it back over. This must be a mistake…

There, my name appears in bold letters. Rosamond June Lynch. No way—this has to be a joke.

After closing the mailbox, I move toward the door. Loud voices echo from the television within, and I hurry to get inside. She must've forgotten how to turn it down again. I rush in to see my grandmother sitting in her favorite brown chair in the living room, unmoved from where I last left her.

Grey hair pulled back in a low bun and in her favorite nightgown. "Grandma, I'm home!"

She doesn't even glance at me as I pass by her to search for the remote. It's gotta be here somewhere. I flip up the cushions on the couch, and it finally reveals itself. I click the power button and stride towards her as she snaps out of her daze. Her weary blue eyes connect with mine, recognition sweeping over her features. "My sweet Rosa. You're home!"

I give her a quick hug and crouch down before her. "I'll make something new for dinner. What did Nurse Meyers give you for lunch?"

A smile forms on her lips, tugging them gently. "O-oh. Ahh, I had chicken. She made me chicken."

"Alright, did she give you your medicine?" Her eyes dart to the left, trying to remember her day. She gives her nod as per usual, like she does every time I ask her about her medicine.

Testing her memory, however, has become a daily ritual. I rise to my feet. "Okay, I will fix something up for you."

She nods once more. "Thank you, dear."

Turning back to the door, I kick off my shoes. The letters in my hand grow heavier and heavier as I proceed into the kitchen. I toss my purse and the letters onto the counter. I'll return to you later. Shaking my head, I sigh, checking the nurse's medical notes. Good.

She ate chicken and took her midday meds. My feet ache, and I want nothing more than a long shower and the comfort of my bedroom by the time I'm done making meatloaf. Once my grandmother is situated and ready for dinner, it takes several minutes of her begging to watch a Hallmark movie for me to give in to her little schemes.

"Fine, alright. But if you watch more tonight, how about you let Nurse Meyer take you on a pleasant walk tomorrow?"

Her eyes brighten. "It's a deal."

I can't help but giggle at the stubborn old woman before me. "Deal! Now, I'm going to go shower. See you soon." I adjust the Hallmark Channel, lowering the volume.

When my eyes meet hers, mischief seeps into her face. "Did you bring back leftover cookies?"

I burst into laughter. "Oh, don't you start with the sweets now. You've gotta eat your meatloaf!"

She sighs with a frown. "A-alright."

I enter the kitchen, grab the letters, and walk down the hall to my room.

Either of these letters could change everything. It could change my life. But how can I leave the only family I have left? And what in the world is Equus Flight Academy...?

* * *

After cleaning up, I sit on my bed and brush a hand through my wet white waves, now flowing loose over my shoulders. The letter in my lap is waiting to be opened. I sigh and grab the first one. My heartbeat quickens. Here goes nothing…

"Dear Rosamond, the Administration Committee of the University of Cincinnati has completed its review of your application. We are grateful for the time you invested in applying for our nursing program. However, we regret to inform you that the committee denied your application. Sincerely, UC."

Heaviness fills my chest. It is, in fact—nothing. I toss the rejection letter across the bed. My only chance of attending a school that I desire close to home…now gone. What am I gonna do now? I shake my head in disbelief as a single tear escapes, running down my cheek. The mysterious envelope still lies in my lap, mocking me. What a cruel joke.

But yet something in me I can't understand wills me to rip it open.

"Dear Rosamond, congratulations. It is with great pleasure that Equus Flight Academy welcomes you into our scholarship program this fall. We apologize that we didn't bring this invitation to your attention sooner, as your father arranged it many years ago. Our

deepest condolences go out to you, and we await a new legacy. We will arrange travel for midday on August 31st. Sincerely, EFA."

My heart pounds, and I whisper aloud. "My father's arrangements? Leave in 2 days?!"

This can't be right…this is some horrible prank.

I toss the paper aside and fall back onto my bed.

After an hour of blankly staring at my ceiling, I make my way back into the living room and sit on the couch. The credits of the movie play, and Grandma's eyes are closed. She purrs, a gentle snore rumbling from her lips.

For a moment, I take in her appearance. Every wrinkle—a story. Memories that have mostly since passed from her mind. Does she know her only son was a student at a mystical school? That he wanted me to follow in his footsteps?

I shake my head at the thought. I'm going insane…there is no mysterious school waiting for me. Time to get Grandma in bed. I get up and gently press her shoulder to wake her and guide her to the room to get ready for the night.

After pulling out her slimy dentures and helping her to the bathroom, I get her tucked into bed. When we say a prayer and she drifts to sleep, I wander back to the kitchen and begin cleaning up.

Exhaustion sweeps over my body, and I yawn deeply mid-dish rinse. Maybe this can wait until tomorrow...

I drag my tired limbs to my room and flop into bed. What am I gonna do? This has to be some cruel mistake—I can't leave her like that.

Chapter 2

A sigh escapes my lips, and I adjust the laptop in front of me. I lay sprawled out on the couch, searching the internet for job openings. So this is what it's come to. I let out a frustrated huff when the computer page reboots again.

Grandma's soft voice trails out from her chair. "Whatever is the matter, my dear?"

I meet her gaze and grab my coffee from the small table before me. "Oh, nothing. Just job hunting. Ready for breakfast?"

Her brows come together in thought. Her sharpest moments are in the morning. And that's when we are happiest together. "Job hunting? But I thought—" Her voice trails off, eyes darting away.

"I didn't get accepted to nursing school." I give her a reassuring smile. "So, now I will look for a job close by. Anything but that blasted diner."

She nods. "I am sorry, hun. If that's what you truly want. Any other offers?"

Everything in me wants to scream. To mourn the life that I could have had here with her, but still pursue my first choice of schooling—to not settle for anything less.

I rise to my feet and sip my coffee. "I think it's for the best. Now, Nurse Meyer will be here shortly. Why don't I fix you up some breakfast before I run some errands?"

She nods and grabs her book and reading glasses from her end table. "Alright."

By the time I'm done scrambling eggs and frying bacon, the doorbell rings, echoing through the house. That's weird… Mrs. Meyers normally knocks and comes in. Years of a daily routine.

"Just a minute!" I call over my shoulder and rinse my hands before striding to the door. I fling it open.

A tall, middle-aged man stands before me. His eyes examine me while I look behind him. Nobody else is there.

"I'm sorry, can I help you?" I demand.

He straightens. "Hello. Are you Ms. Lynch?"

How does this stranger know my name? My heartbeat quickens, and before I know it, I'm slamming the door shut.

He places a firm hand on the door before I can shut it. "Ms. Lynch. I'm from Equus Flight Academy. At your father's request, I'm here to escort you."

My hands freeze on the door. "You're what…?" I snap.

"Here to escort you to the Academy." His voice is calm and collected despite my reaction.

I open the door wider to see more of him. Black and purple activewear clings to his arms despite his age. Specks of gray glint in his brown hair. "Is that so? How am I supposed to believe a stranger?"

The stranger smirks. "He said you'd probably say something like that."

I swallow hard. "Who?"

"Your father. I must say, you're the spitting image of him. Those bright green eyes. Now, is that delightful mother of his around? June, correct?" His voice is chipper and confident.

I nod, speechless. He knows her name…? He knew my father?

He extends a hand. "My apologies, I'm Henry. I was a close friend of your father, Jack, during our time at the Academy."

I take a step back, and he smiles softly. "May I come in? Your grandmother and I should be able to clear everything up for you."

I shake my head and open the door, barely forming the

words that roll out of my mouth. "My grandma has dementia—I don't think she would be very helpful at the moment. But follow me."

Henry looks at me in surprise before I lead him to the living room and gesture for him to take a seat on the couch. "You can sit here."

I turn my attention to my grandmother, who is oblivious to us, still deep in her book. "Grandma, someone is here to see us," I say, snapping her from her concentration.

June's eyes scan around the room before focusing on the man sitting down. Her eyes widen, shock seeping into her wrinkled face. "I–I don't know what to say. Is that you?"

My jaw nearly falls open. This is real…this conversation is happening.

She sets her book aside and smiles at him. "It's been ages! How are you, dear boy?"

Henry straightens and smiles at her. "I'm hardly a boy anymore," he teases before clearing his throat. "But I am so very sorry for your loss. Your son was a good man."

Grandma June's lips part as if she wants to say more, but Henry's words cut her short. "Ms. Lynch, may I have a word alone with your grandmother to discuss a few details?"

I shift uncomfortably and face her. "I guess so. Grandma, are you okay with that?"

She nods her approval, and I turn to leave but spin around. "I'm not going far, and I will monitor you both."

Henry smiles. "As you should. This will only take a moment, thank you."

I stride into the kitchen and listen to hushed tones from the other room. After a couple of moments, every muscle tenses as I creep back to the edge of the living room, just out of sight.

I peer around the wall in time to see the man rise from his seat again and lace his fingers together. "It is time to take her to EFA."

Grandma June's brows furrow together. "Oh, is it that time already? I had nearly forgotten!"

Forgotten? The little rascal never said a word to me. I stand there speechless, unable to process this information. I'm not going anywhere, and I'm certainly not going with this guy. I huff in frustration.

Her soft blue eyes find mine in seconds, and I force my limbs back into the living room.

"Rosa, you must go with him. Find your place there—as your father did," she says, just as confident as this man Henry is acting.

I swallow the lump in my throat. She kept a secret from me? Anger stirs in my chest. "Grandma, excuse my language, but I didn't even know my sorry excuse of a father. How can you say that? How can I leave you alone here?" I huff in disbelief. "I won't. This is ridiculous!"

June's eyes narrow. "Watch your tone, young lady. We—have a guest." She snaps.

Henry steps forward. "I will ensure she gets the care she needs. However, I can make this transition easier. It's what Jack would've wanted."

And there he goes again, using my father's name. The father I never knew. The father who abandoned Mom and me eighteen years ago.

Rage explodes in my chest, and I direct it at him. "Well, in that case, I'm sure he wouldn't have wanted me to leave my grandma here like this. Can't you see that?" I hold my stare.

Henry steps closer. "Your father wanted this, though he didn't know these circumstances would complicate it."

I close my eyes and take a breath before turning back to her. "Grandma, why are you both so determined that I go? Don't you want me to stay with you?"

Blue eyes brighten as she takes me in. "There is much you do not understand, but do you trust me, dear?"

I shake my head. "Yes, of course I do! But—"

She lifts her chin. "You must. I'll be alright; go pack your bag."

Shifting uncomfortably, I stare at my feet for a long moment before lifting my eyes. "Fine, I'll go. But on one condition: I can come back whenever I want, and if it doesn't work out, no hard feelings."

Henry's eyes lock into mine. "Fair enough. I'm happy to see your father's plans through but if it doesn't work out in the end that's okay."

My stomach churns as I glance back at her. "Why didn't he try to make contact before he passed? Is this really what my father wanted?" I ask.

To those questions, they answer in unison. "Yes, Rosamond."

Chapter 3

I kneel in piles of clothes, letting out a sigh of frustration. What do I even bring to this place? I stuff as many outfits as I can into my duffel bag and some toiletries, then slide on a black hooded sweatshirt and jeans.

What else? What else?

Pressing my fingers to my chin, I stride over to the mirror. My messy hair covers my shoulders, and I pull it back into a ponytail. Turning to grab my charger, I slip my phone into my back pocket. Here goes nothing…

By the time I make it to the hallway, voices echo from the living room. Nurse Meyers! I hurry my pace, and they all turn to me when I enter the room.

Henry stands up from the couch again. "Are you ready to go? I have just made all the arrangements for your Grandma June with Nurse Meyers while we waited." He tries to reassure me.

I set my bag down and walk closer to her chair. "Are you

sure you want me to go? I can stay." I plead with my eyes.

She shakes her head before a smile spreads across her lips. "It is all for the best, my dear. GO."

Bending down, I wrap my arms around her. "I'll miss you so much. I love you!"

Her wrinkled arms hold me tight. "I love you too, Rosa."

She pulls back and pats my hand. "Now get going. And don't you worry about me. I'll be fine."

The walk…what about her exercise?

"Remember our deal? You agreed to a pleasant walk today." I breathe.

The nurse smiles and takes June's arm to help her get ready. Grandma's blue eyes lock into mine, and she smiles. "See you soon, I love you so much."

My heart hammers in my chest, and tears threaten my eyes. "I love you too—see you soon." My throat tightens, and that's all I manage to get out.

* * *

The car hits a pothole, sending a jolt through my body in the backseat of the black sedan. "Where exactly is this academy?" I call out to Henry in the driver's seat.

He chuckles as if amused by my confusion. "In the mountainous terrain of Colorado."

My mouth hangs open. "Colorado? As in half across the country..?"

His smile reflects in the rear-view mirror. "Yes, and we are almost at the airport."

This guy clearly isn't from around here. "We already passed the airport—you'll have to turn around."

He shakes his head. "No, not that airport."

I brush the strand of hair out of my face. "W-hat airport then?"

"You'll see," he says.

I try not to bombard him with questions and sit quietly.

After a few minutes of silence, he pulls into a driveway that's posted. Private Property. I'm not so sure that this is legal... "Are you sure you know where you're going?" I finally speak up.

He chuckles again. "You'll just have to find out. You know, you remind me a lot of your dad. So many questions."

I shrug. "Didn't know the guy. Walked out on us when I was little."

Henry falls quiet at my abrupt statement, but I'm thankful the small talk is over. So I let the awkward silence linger until an open field comes into view with a private jet on a small runway.

I can't help but chime in quietly. "Ahh. This airport…"

"Mmm-hmm." He almost hums.

Henry pulls the car right up to the plane on the pavement. "Your first flight at EFA awaits." He muses.

I grab my bag and pull it close. "First flight?"

"You'll get that one—later." He turns and winks at me before getting out and opening my door.

Here goes nothing…

I stand and follow him to the side of the plane and stride up the stairs into the jet. He turns around. "It's gonna be a long flight. Go make yourself comfortable."

In seconds he's gone behind a curtain into the front of the plane. I throw my bag into the overhead compartment to my right and watch as the stairs fold up and seal back into the jet. Fancy.

My heartbeat quickens at the roar of the engine, and I find my way to a seat and buckle in.

Equus Flight Academy, here I come…

Chapter 4

I shift in my seat five hours later and pick at the small bowl of peanuts next to my empty dinner plate. I'm about to get up again when Henry's voice echoes over the radio. "Prepare for landing. Please stay seated."

I grumble to myself. "Finally!" I can't wait to be back on the ground.

The airplane dips to the left, and we begin our descent. I open the tiny window shade all the way to see puffy clouds passing by as the mountainous landscape unfolds.

The enormous stone-pillared academy and grounds come into view, and I nearly gasp, leaning closer to the window.

It's like something straight out of medieval times. The grounds around the massive buildings fan out into perfectly arranged gardens and miles of fenced-in pasture.

My eyes catch the giant dome behind the academy. What in the world is that? I snap out of my daze and realize we are heading straight towards a small runway between a thick row of trees. The plane dips again, and I grasp the armrests.

We plummet to the ground, my stomach churning, and I squeeze my eyes shut as the jet collides with the landing strip. My whole body jolts forward as the brakes screech, bringing us to a stop after a few moments.

I fling my eyes open and let out the breath I had been holding. Once I'm sure we aren't going anywhere else, I unbuckle and get my duffel.

Henry emerges from behind the curtain, his smile reaching his eyes. "Welcome to EFA! Come with me."

At his last words, the stairs of the jet unfold and fresh mountain air pours in. I adjust my sweatshirt and grip my bag tighter.

He must see the panic on my face. "Breathe kid. This isn't even the fun part yet." He teases.

Is he always this cheerful? I shrug and feel my cheeks flush. "So, what next?" I ask.

He strides down the stairs and calls over his shoulder. "Admissions office. Let's get you checked in and get everything settled."

I hurry and follow him out of the plane. "What will housing look like—"

A loud blaring horn sounds in the distance as a boy driving the biggest golf cart I've ever seen whips around the corner, cutting off my words. The maniac drives at full speed, heading straight for us. I step behind Henry in a lazy attempt to shield myself and peek out from behind him when the cart skids to a stop before us. Henry looks at me, eyes full of excitement. "Hop in!"

There is no way I'm letting that reckless kid drive me anywhere. I straighten my back. "Only if...you drive."

He eyes the boy with blond hair and sighs. Disappointment seeps into the kid's face, but he slides out of the cart and sits in the backseat.

Henry waves a hand. "Alright, let's go."

I take my seat beside him on the passenger side and pull my bag onto my lap. At that, we peel off in the direction from which the boy came. We round the bend and after a few minutes, we reach the main entrance to the Academy.

The boy speaks up when we pass under a large stone archway. "Did you know that there is a super cool shield that prevents the outside world from seeing us?! I couldn't believe it when I first got here!"

"Huh?" I mutter.

"My name is Aidan." He blurts out.

I shift in my seat and turn to face him. "I'm Rosam—" I clear my throat and smile. "Rosa. Nice to meet you."

He grins. "Oh, I know. Was just introducing myself."

What? I swallow hard. "What do you mean…you know?"

He waves a hand as if unbothered by my question. "It's not every day that a legacy shows up."

That's right. "A legacy…" I turn forward just as Henry pulls the cart up in front of the Academy. The boy—Aidan—hops out and strides through the main double doors of the tall, cathedral-looking building to my left. I grab my duffel and turn to get out.

At the front of the academy, a Pegasus statue made of stone captivates me. It stands on its hind legs with wings outstretched into the air. Neatly arranged gardens fan out behind it in the distance. This is cool…

Henry clears his throat. "Come on, let's get you checked in."

I whip my head in his direction, heat rising to my cheeks. "A-alright."

I nod and follow him through the main entrance.

Quickening my pace behind him, I pass through hallways and by several enormous staircases. Students pass us in the hall, some even peek out from classrooms, curious about the newcomer.

My stomach turns when a pair of girls gawk at me as they pass by, eyeing me from head to toe with disgust. Great. It can't be worse than high school…can it? I set my focus forward, willing myself not to look at anyone else.

Henry abruptly stops before me and opens a door to the right. "Here we are." He breathes.

I take a shaky breath and follow him in.

A middle-aged woman with shoulder-length blond hair rises from a seat at her desk. "Ah–Ms. Lynch. We've been expecting you. My name is Ms. Charlotte."

I smile at her. "Nice to meet you."

Henry clasps his hands together and gives her a toothy grin. "Rosa needs to be checked into the system and a room found for her stay."

Ms. Charlotte sits back down. "Yes, of course." She types vigorously on the computer keyboard.

"Okay, all set." She stands again, her brown eyes meeting mine. "You will be in room twenty-seven. In the west wing. I have arranged a meeting in the morning before breakfast at eight to go over the scholarship details and class schedule."

I step forward. "Scholarship details?"

She gives Henry a look that I can't quite distinguish, and he clears his throat. Something is off…

Before I can insist upon them telling me what is wrong, he turns on his heel and strides back out the door. I smile at Ms. Charlotte and hurry to catch up with him. "Hey–what was that about?" I prod.

He slows his pace and glances down at me. "Not something you need to worry about right now. Let's get you to your room." He gestures to the hall.

I shake my head. "If you insist."

We stride down hallway after hallway back towards the main doors. He stops at a wide set of stairs and spins around, pinning his arms behind his back. "Up you go. Follow the stairs to the right at the split. Second floor. Room twenty-seven."

I shrug and look up at him. "I know I'm not supposed to ask again…but what is this all about?"

He sighs. "I wish your father could've seen you here. You know, it would've made him so happy."

I shift uncomfortably. "You know more about my dad than I do. I'm afraid—"

Henry clears his throat. "Why don't you just get settled in your room, and we'll talk in the morning."

My chest tightens, but I nod.

He turns to leave and calls over his shoulder. "Breakfast is at eight sharp in the cafeteria. Your roommate will show you the way."

My roommate? My heart pounds, and I call after him. "You said nothing about a roommate—"

He's gone as I fumble out my last words. What is with these people? Gripping my duffel bag, I face the stairs. Here goes nothing…

Chapter 5

I knock on the door that has a golden twenty-seven on it and then pull my hand away. Footsteps from within grow closer, and I take a shaky breath.

The door swings open, and a girl only a couple of inches taller than me stands there, her big brown eyes meeting mine. She brushes a strand of short, raven hair behind her ear. Black and purple athletic clothing clings to her muscled legs and arms.

This girl is oddly intimidating, and I just stare at her momentarily, forgetting what it is I'm supposed to say. She shifts her weight to one side and peeks around me as if annoyed. "Ah—can I help you?" She asks.

I snap out of it and fling out my hand. "I'm Rosa. Your roommate, I guess."

Her brows furrow and she scoffs. "Mmm. That's right. So, you're the legacy, huh?" She stretches out her hand to meet mine. "The name's Jamie. Come in." She steps back as

I enter the room.

It's surprisingly big, and I take in the two beds on opposite sides. Wooden dressers are underneath two large windows, and a desk is in another corner next to a mini-fridge.

She turns and picks up a bottle of water from a small round table centered in the middle of the dorm.

I scratch my neck. "Cozy…"

Jamie crosses her arms over her chest. "Isn't it nice? Because of the scholarship program, the school has too many students. Second-years and above typically have their own room. First-year students and scholarship applicants are on the first floor, but you got lucky. Me—not so much."

She wasn't supposed to have a roommate. Subtle. "You're a second-year?" I glance to the right side of the bedroom, littered with her stuff. "When did you get in?"

Jamie clears her throat. "Yeah, I made it onto the flight team. Got here weeks ago. My mom was itching for me to leave, and so she pulled a few strings."

I meet her eyes, now full of curiosity. "Are you on scholarship?"

"Oh, no, my parents are paying my way through. You?" She says without hesitation.

I shake my head. Must be nice. "On scholarship. Speaking

of which, what is the deal with that?"

She pulls a sweatshirt on. "Just some silly old competition they put on every four years so that someone can win a scholarship."

I swallow a lump forming in my throat. "W-win...? Competition?"

"Yup, everybody knows that." Jamie strides to the door, and I stand there speechless.

Did she say competition?

She sips her water. "You'll get used to it. Catch you later, Rosa." She says, leaving the room.

I run a hand over my hair and sigh. Nobody had said anything about a competition. The left side of the room is empty...ready to claim my name. I walk over and peer out the window just as the sun sets below the trees, pinks and purples peeking through.

I yawn and grab my duffel, approaching the bed made up in simple white linen. Tossing my bag at the dresser close by, I kick off my sneakers and lie back on the bed. Grandma June's words echo in my mind. "Find your place there—just like your father did."

I picture her blue eyes and sweet smile. Tears well up in my eyes, taking me by surprise.

This is all wrong. How can I stay here?

I can't do this.

***

An obnoxious sound rings in my ears, and I roll over. Alarm clock. Sunlight spills through the bottom of the windows, now concealed by a curtain. I groan and grab a pillow, covering my head. Make it stop!

The ringing fades, and Jamie's footsteps sound across the floor. "You'd better get up, too. Don't wanna miss breakfast."

I groan again and lift my head. "W-what time is it?"

"Almost eight. Better hurry." She huffs.

I shoot straight up. "Already? When did I fall asleep?" Jamie raises a brow. "You were out like a light when I got back. Oh, and you definitely wanna change…I'm sure they'll give you your training clothes soon enough."

I rub my tired eyes. "Huh?"

She sighs in annoyance. "Oh, never mind! I'll wait for you if you hurry. Meet me at the bottom of the stairs after you change."

She zips up her fitted purple and black long-sleeve shirt and strides out the door.

Crap. The meeting...

I scramble out of bed and sort through my clothing bag. Light jeans and a grey t-shirt catch my eye. Good enough. I slip on the clean clothes and fix my ponytail before rushing out the door. Strolling to the bathroom in the hall, I freshen up before hurrying down the stairs.

Jamie rolls her eyes when I reach the bottom of the staircase. "It took you that long to change into that?" She grumbles.

I stop mid-stride. "Hey! What's wrong with what I'm wearing?" I frown. "I have to get back to Ms. Charlotte's office for a meeting. Please show me the way?"

She turns on her heel, waving her hand in the air. "Oh—come on!"

I keep in step with her strides, grateful that she's showing me the way. Students spill into the hallway, all going in the same direction.

After a few minutes, she slows down, pointing her finger at a door on the right. "Here's your stop. The cafeteria is just down the hall to the right."

I smile. "Thanks, Jamie. See you later."

"Don't mention it." She smirks and takes off down the hall to what I'd assume is the cafe from the sweet aroma hanging in the air.

Chapter 6

Straightening my shirt, I enter the Headmistress's office. Henry sits in a chair in front of Ms. Charlotte's desk. "Good morning!" He says cheerfully, and he motions for me to sit in the other chair beside him.

I take the seat and smile sheepishly. "Good morning."

Turning my attention to the woman at the desk, she meets my gaze. "Hello again, Ms. Lynch. Are you ready to discuss the terms of our scholarship program? Or, better referred to as our competition."

I look at Henry's intense green gaze before flicking my eyes back to her. He said nothing about there being terms.

"The terms?" I ask.

Ms. Charlotte straightens in her chair. "Every four years the academy offers a chance for ten students to compete against each other for a full-ride scholarship."
Gesturing with her hand, she continues. "You see, your father long ago won this competition. And was a significant

influence here at EFA. Now, we are offering you the same chance to ride in this competition. To win."

A knot twists in my stomach. "Ride? I have never even been on the back of a horse…"

Laughter bubbles from her lips, and she briefly glances at Henry before turning her attention back to me. "Oh, dear. Didn't he tell you? You will not only be riding but you'll be flying a Pegasus to compete."

Henry clears his throat. "After all, it wouldn't be called Equus Flight School for nothing!"

They chuckle in unison, and my blood boils.

I rise from my seat, turning to face him. "You didn't care to mention all this before I got here?" I demand.

"If you knew, you wouldn't have come…" He says.

"Yeah," I say with a huff. "Pretty much…this is all part of some crazy dream, right?"

His face softens. "It's what your father wanted. For you to get accustomed to the idea slowly. I'm sorry for all the secrecy."

I cross my arms over my chest. "Is that so?"

Charlotte stands at her desk, holding out a paper to me. "Here is your schedule, Rosamond."

I reach out and take it from her. "My schedule?"

Henry chimes in before she can answer. "Yes. You will have

classes to attend as well as a lot of physical training to do before the first trial race in three weeks."

She sits back down at her desk, and I glance down at the paper in my hands. Classes with detailed times and room numbers fill the page. Trial race. "There's a trial race?"

She clasps her hands, resting them on the desk. "It is to give the students practice before they face one of the biggest challenges. There will be two trial races before the ultimate competition."

I take a breath. "I don't know what to say…" Charlotte smiles, then types at her computer. "Classes start Monday. The day after tomorrow. One more thing, what size training clothes would you like sent to your room, Rosamond?"

This is happening. This is crazy…

"Small—and call me Rosa," I say.

"Will do, Rosa." She breathes.

Henry stands beside me. "Why don't we get you some food? Take some time to adjust to the news."

I nod and fold the schedule before slipping it into my pocket.

****

The cafeteria is crowded by the time I find it. Almost everyone is sitting with his or her tray of food, chatting. In the back of the room, there is a large buffet of food, and I weave through the sea of black and purple to reach it.

As I search for something to eat, I feel their eyes heavily on me, but I try to ignore them. Whatever invisible charm I had in high school is thrown out the window now—here—I'm the legacy.

After grabbing a couple of items, I turn to find a seat as a lanky boy with blond hair strides right towards me. Aidan—not him again. He's already spotted me, and there's no time to escape.

The kid reaches me in seconds, face beaming with excitement. "Hey there!"

I smile politely. "Hi."

"If you're looking for a place to sit, my table's open."

"Uhh. Well."

He's one of the few people I know right now…

"Sure," I say.

Aidan turns, and I follow him through the maze of tables to

an empty one in the corner.

His table is literally open as he had said because there is nobody else here. I kind of feel bad for the guy. Looking over my shoulder, I scan the room to find Jamie.

A few eyes lock into mine, but I ignore them and finally spot her sitting across the room. Laughter shakes her body, and she hits the boy next to her. So she does laugh…

I turn back to the almost fully empty table facing the wall and take a seat across from Aidan.

"So, if you want, I could show you around after we eat?" He asks, snapping me out of my thoughts.

"Hmm? Oh yeah, that would be great." I nod. "I'm struggling to find my way around."

He pops crackers into his bowl of steaming chili. "Wait till you see the Pegasus! I have been working here at the stables since the summer. They're awesome!"

Who is this guy?

"Wait, so you're not a student here?" I ask.

"Nope, just a stable-hand. I also help with odds and ends here and there, hence the chauffeur thing."

That explains a lot. My mind replays the image of Aidan driving the go-kart at full speed like a lunatic. I stifle a bubble of laughter, but it threatens to escape, so I pick at the salad on my plate, hoping that'll help distract me. This kid is something else.

He shifts in his seat, the silence between us seeming to bother him. "Uh—did you know this academy has been around for one hundred years?!"

I try to pay attention to his words, but his perkiness is annoyingly distracting. "C-cool. Two days ago, I didn't know about this place."

"Yup! I know all about that." He insists.

I raise an eyebrow, cutting in. "You seem to know a lot about me—you are kind of freaking me out a little."

He waves his hand in a dismissive gesture. "Everyone knows about you being a legacy, that is, no big deal. You know, after the first trial race, there will be a dance to celebrate the school's anniversary. You should join in the fun; the stable hands can come!"

I can't help but smile at the lanky kid in front of me, part of me grateful for his cheery distraction now. "Still getting used to that fact, I guess. I'll think about the anniversary thing, just need to focus on getting through the first couple of days here."

We sit in awkward silence and finish our food. With his last bite, he stands and lifts his tray.

"Ready for that tour? I can offer you a small one before I have to get back to work."

I grab my tray and stand. "Sounds like a plan."

We discard our trays at the counter, avoiding the gawking students as we pass back through and exit the room. Relief floods me when no more prying eyes are on my back, and I look to Aidan. "Where to first?" I ask.

He scratches his chin. "I'll show you the most direct path to the arena and stables! Some of your classes will be on the first floor in this building, but most will be out back."

I nod. "Oh-okay."
He starts down the hallway at a speedy pace, and I try to follow. After a few minutes of passing through hallways, we reach the double doors at the back of the building.

A knot twists in my stomach when he flings his body against the door, pushing it open.

Here we go…

Chapter 7

The large domed structure looms in the distance, followed by several stables and pastures lining each side, disappearing behind it.

I take a deep breath as my eyes roam over all the Pegasus grazing in the fields, all of different colors and sizes. Giant wings tucked in, lying flat against their sides. They're amazing and I almost can't believe what I'm seeing. It's like nothing I've ever seen before…

Aidan looks over his shoulder, taking in my reaction. "Most magical thing you've ever seen, right?" He says, wonder and awe fill his brown eyes.

I nod, and my heart quickens at the sight of these beautiful creatures. "Mm-hmm!" I agree.

My eyes settle back on the gigantic dome central to everything around it. "What's that?"

He notes the direction of my gaze and turns. "Oh. That—yeah. The main training arena. It's enclosed so that

39

first-years can do most of their training there at the beginning. Or so I'm told."

I walk towards the pasture on my left. "Gotcha."

A medium-sized white horse—Pegasus—stands close to the dark wooden fence, capturing my attention.

Aidan calls out from behind me. "I've gotta get back to work! Go enjoy!"

"Okay, see you later," I call out, waving to him before I turn back to the pasture. The Pegasus lifts its head from the luscious grass as I approach. "Hi." I breathe.

The white-muscled animal takes a step closer and rests its long face over the fence. What a beauty. I reach my hand out slowly and breathe in when its long nose tilts up to meet my hand. Its face is soft and warm. My eyes catch on a grey marking that resembles a crescent moon between her bright green eyes.

"She likes you." A familiar voice rings out behind me.

I jump as the Pegasus startles back, and I whip around to see Henry, a smile spreading across his lips. "Sorry to sneak up on you; it looked like you were having a good time."

"I–ah. Yes, I was." I turn back to the beauty behind the fence. "What's her name?"

He steps closer, gesturing with his hand. "Stardust. This is her first official year at the academy."

Hmm, Stardust. I like that. "She's beautiful—"

Henry chuckles. "I think you'll settle in just fine. On that note, I have something for you."

I turn to face him again. "What?"

He runs a hand through his hair and pulls a letter from his pocket. "I forgot to give you this earlier. Your father had written a letter for you to read after your arrival here." Henry clears his throat. "You should have it."

My heart sinks at the mention of my father, and I step forward and take the letter from him. "Thanks." I gaze down at my supposed father's handwriting. "This really was all part of some crazy plan of his, huh?"

I sigh, continuing my thoughts. "Sometimes I wish I'd gotten the chance to meet him."

He nods. "Yes, yes. Now you take time to rest and adjust to everything today before training starts tomorrow."

I nod in agreement. "Thanks again for the letter. And I will." We just stare at each other. This is awkward, and time is dragging on forever.

Henry clears his throat again. "My pleasure. Well, see you later, kid."

We part ways, and I grip the letter tightly in my hand. Tears threaten my eyes, and I hurry back down the path from which we came.

Slowing my pace, I wander the halls and find the stairs that lead to my room. As I approach the staircase, a pretty girl with straight brown hair strides down. Her hazel eyes lift to mine, and she glares. "Get out of my way." She growls.

I step back in surprise. "S-sorry." I stutter. Her eyes narrow at me as she passes.

"I didn't know you owned the stairs," I mumble under my breath. She stops and swings around, her angry eyes colliding with mine.

"Excuse me? What did you just say to me?" She snaps.

Wrong thing to say. "Nothing." I shrug.

"That's what I thought. I'm Tess Fletcher. My father practically owns this school, actually." She flicks her hair over her shoulder. "I don't care that you're some stupid legacy, okay? Stay out of my way!"

Well, then. Turning away, I sigh. "Duly noted. Sorry."

Day one and I'm already making enemies…great. I take the stairs two at a time and rush into the dorm. Jamie is nowhere to be seen. What does she do all the time?

I kick off my shoes and plop onto my bed, but a large box sits on the table, catching my attention. I set the letter on my bed and head towards the mysterious box.

Before I reach the table, Jamie bursts through the door. "Oh. You're back." She notes my gaze. "A box of training clothes showed up for you while you were out."

I step closer to the table and take in the box that's partially opened. "You snooped? It has my name on it…" She shrugs her shoulders. "It was just training clothes."

I cross my arms. "I see that. But whatever, it's fine." "It's not a big deal. Anyway, are you coming to the party at the cliff tonight?"

"What? A cliff?" I sigh. "No, thanks." She strides across the room, grabbing a soda from the mini-fridge. "Your loss. I knew you were gonna be a goody two-shoes."

The nerve of this girl! What is her problem?

"I am not! Really, I need to unpack and call my grandma back home."

She bursts into a humorless laugh. "You know, you are only proving my last point more and more."

I choke back a laugh. "Hey—" She plops onto her bed and slips her headphones on, her attention now fixed on the screen in her hand. Well, I guess our conversation is over. I grab the box full of clothes and sit on the floor next to my dresser.

By the time I'm done sorting through the black and purple athletic wear and putting it away, Jamie stands and tosses her headphones back onto the bed.

"I'm going to lunch." She slips on her shoes and strides out the door within seconds.

I shake my head. Bye…

Grabbing my duffel, I finish putting everything away. There. That's better. I glance over at my bed.

The letter.

I get up from the floor and lie back on my bed. Holding up the envelope with my father's handwriting on it and I let my finger trace each word. I can't read this. Not now.

I roll to my side, dropping it from my hands. Part of me desperately wants to know after all this time, the other half of me wants to hate him forever.

I'm not ready to read his words yet…not by a long shot.

Chapter 8

After dinner, I make my way back up the stairs to my dorm. Aidan chatted my ear off the entire time, and Tess shot me too many glares from afar. I'm ready for some peace.

Once in my room, I grab my phone and sit at the table. Grandma's probably starting another Hallmark by now, fiddling with the TV remote. I bring my knees to my chest in the metal chair and dial the home number.

After a moment, it goes to voicemail. I clear my froggy throat. "Hi Grandma, it's Rosa. Just wanted to call and tell you I arrived safely at the academy. And–ah, just call me back when you get this message. Love you! Bye."

I rest my arms on my knees and sigh. This is around the time she'd be drifting off in her cozy chair after dinner as a movie plays. My chest aches at the thought of her being alone. But the nurses will take good care of her, right?

I have to keep telling myself that...

Jamie slips in the door and stops in front of me, eyeing me up and down. "Are you okay there?"

I fidget with my hair, tucking a strand behind my ear. "Yeah. I just wasn't able to get a hold of my grandma. I—miss her."

She places a hand on her hip. "You just got here…"

"Well, I'm used to being with her a lot. I'm sure she feels the same way." I insist.

"Mmm. I'm sure my family doesn't miss me like that." She says flatly, turning away.

My heart sinks. "Why do you say that?"

Jamie straightens her shoulders and turns to face me again. "Oh, come on! Let's not get all mushy-gushy. I've gotta get ready for the party."

"Yeah—the cliff party." I tease.

"Oh, stop! You sure you don't wanna come?"

I raise an eyebrow. "Are you warming up to the idea of sharing a dorm or something?"

She shakes her head. "Never…" Sarcasm lingers in her tone.

I get up. "Just checking. Besides, don't we have training early tomorrow?"

She turns and walks over to her dresser. "Yeah, yeah. It'll be fine."

"Well, I'm going to lie down." I grab my green pajama set along with my toiletry bag and head for the door.

"You have fun…for me." I call over my shoulder and head to the bathroom.

* * *

My heart races. I know this isn't real—not anymore—but everything in me wants to scream and call out for my mom in the front seat of the SUV. The truck slams into the driver's side. Glass shatters. I scream from the back and clutch my seatbelt. I can't breathe. No! There is a ringing sound in my ears.

I sit up in bed, panting for air with tears streaming down my face. Just a dream. It's over now—a dream.

I rub the scar on my shoulder. Faint moonlight spills into the room, casting it into shadows, and I look around. No Jamie. She must still be at the party.

I slide out of bed, put on my slippers, and head to the bathroom sink. My muscles relax when I splash cool water on my face, and I sigh, using my shirt as a towel. Messy hair flows over my shoulders, and bloodshot eyes meet me in the mirror. I need to get out. Fresh air—something.

I don't remember deciding to, but I force my tired limbs down the stairs and out the main doors. A cool breeze whips through my pajamas, and I suck in a breath, making my way past the Pegasus statue and into the front gardens.

Faded lampposts give little light, and I squint my eyes to keep going. A small stone bench comes into view, and I decide that's my target. Perfect…

It's cold on my legs as I sit, but the mountain air is so refreshing. Breathing deeply, I tilt my head back, looking up at a million stars painting the sky. I've never seen stars like this…so bright and clear out here. I sit for a few moments, or perhaps an hour, my mind wandering.

Until a branch cracks behind me, snapping me out of my thoughts.

"Hey, I've got this bench tonight. Well, every night to be exact." A charming voice calls out from behind me.

I lunge forward and spin around, my heart catching in my throat. "W-what? Who is there?"

I squint to make out a boy's figure a few feet away.

He chuckles. "I didn't mean to scare you. But this is my spot."

My heart beats faster at the sound of his laugh. "Oh. How

many students think they own this school? I'm new here, so I didn't know."

As he steps closer, his features become more distinct. I take in his short black hair and slim but muscular build. Though his eyes hide in the shadows, making their color impossible to discern, my breath hitches.

A shiver crawls up my spine as I look at him. He's cute…

"Did you lose your way or something?" He asks abruptly, pulling me out of my thoughts. I was gazing intently at him for way too long.

My cheeks flush as I shake my head. "I just wanted to go outside, actually." I needed fresh air.
"The stars here are truly breathtaking. I've never seen anything like it." I insist.

He is silent for a moment and tilts his head to the sky. "I see. I'm Nate, by the way."

I swallow hard. "Rosa."
He stares, taking in my pajamas. My heart skips, and I want nothing more than to disappear from his heavy gaze.

"I know who you are, Legacy."

I tuck a strand of wild hair behind my ear. "Oh, wait, of course you know who I am!"

I sigh. "Well, Nate. I'll leave you to your bench."
I'm beginning to hate this label everyone seems so

delighted to give me.

He remains silent, and before this attractive stranger has time to reply, I hurry back towards the academy, guided by the dim lampposts and starlight.

Chapter 9

Jamie strides across the room to her dresser. A groan escapes her lips for the third time. I can't help but giggle. "How's that cliff party treating you right about now?"

She grumbles. "Oh, shut it!" A small grin tugs at the corner of her mouth. "Okay—you were right. Partying the night before training. Should have remembered that from last year."

I can't help but smile back and grab the training clothes from my dresser. "We'd better hurry. Don't wanna be late." I put on the black riding pants and tank top, then grab the purple and black spandex zip-up.

I glance at Jamie lacing up her black ankle boots. "Where did you get those?" I motion to her shoes.

She shrugs. "Didn't they give you a pair already?"

I shake my head. "Oh. Um, no. I didn't get any yet."

She finishes lacing them up and stands. "I guess you can

use my extra pair for now. Don't get used to it, though. You need to get your own pair. I'm seven and a half. You?"

She clearly intends to intimidate others with her appearance. Her dark, short hair contrasts with her brown eyes, which are emphasized by heavy eyeliner.

But she is lightening up to me, right? I swallow.

"I'm a size seven. That should be okay for now, thanks." She grabs her extra pair of boots and tosses them to my side of the room before striding to the door.
"See you at the stable after breakfast." She calls out, her voice fading into the hall.

With Jamie gone, I lace up the boots and slide on my long sleeve, zipping the collar up my neck. I sigh at the surprising comfort of the uniform, even though it's the tightest clothing I've ever worn. I tie my hair up in a high ponytail and turn to leave, but the white envelope on my dresser catches my eye. My father's letter.

I stride back over and grab it. I've got to read it eventually… I carefully rip it open.

"My dear little Rosamond,

Everything happened so suddenly. I wish I had been there when your mother died. As much as I try to make excuses for what I did…leaving you both is unforgivable. The worst mistake of my life. But I have little time left, and I am so sorry to leave you with only this.

I begged the nurse to give me a pen and paper so I could write these words to you. It's gonna be okay.

There is no easy way to tell you this, but I had been keeping a secret. A piece of my past I kept hidden, even from your mother. After your eighteenth birthday, the academy will contact you.

A man named Henry will take care of all the arrangements for you to go there when you come of age. He was my best friend, you can trust him. Equus Flight Academy changed my life, and I'm so sorry I won't be there to show you everything that I learned.

Go to the academy. Train and win the competition. The first year is hard, but don't give up. Rosa, you are so much stronger than you think. I know you can do it. One day I know you will soar through the sky just like I did. I will always love you, Dad."

I dab at the tear rolling down my face before I recall letting it fall and study the letter further. Words become blurrier by the second. All this time he loved me? He really wanted this for me?

Next to it, I grab my class schedule, dropping the letter back on my dresser.

If I'm gonna make it here, I'll need to train hard so that I can earn my place. Turning, I rush out the door to the cafeteria.

*　*　*

I pass the dome arena and hurry my pace after spotting a group of twenty students standing by a fence in the distance. Two people are giving instructions in the front, and I sneak into the group from the back and find Jamie.

She tilts her head, raven hair catching in the breeze. "Cutting it close, don't you think?" My friend whispers.

I shrug and peek between a few students ahead. "What are you doing here?"

She smirks. "Came to see all the action."

Henry stands at the front, alongside a guy—with short black hair—my heart catches in my throat. It's the stranger from last night? What is he doing up there?

I'm still in disbelief when—Nate—clears his throat and

addresses the group. "I'm Nate! I'll be assisting Coach Henry this year and heading up most of the training for the scholarship applicants." His voice is steady and authoritative, unlike his tone last night.

Henry clasps his hands together. "Now, before we divide into two groups. Here comes the fun part!"
He gestures to the field of Pegasus behind him before continuing. "Both first-year students and scholarship applicants will pair up with a Pegasus! Though instead of you choosing them. They get to choose you!" He beams.

What? How are they going to choose us?

My throat goes dry. Nate lifts his arm and points to the gate lining the fence. "Each of you, one at a time, will walk into the pasture and let a Pegasus choose you. However, if you don't get chosen—you're cut. Everyone, go line up over there." He commands.

I stayed instead of running back home, and now I have to get chosen? How is this fair?

A boy with shaggy brown hair speaks up. "Wait, we are supposed to just walk out into the field full of Pegasus and hope that one chooses us before we get trampled?"

Nate turns his attention to the boy. "Yes. If that poses a problem and anxiety gets the best of you, then perhaps you don't belong here." He turns to address the group. "Again, who will go first?"

I hear myself speak before I know what I'm doing. "Uh–I will." I say.

Everyone whips their heads around to me. What did I just do? I'm an idiot…

I step forward. It's too late now to pretend it wasn't me who just volunteered. I clear my throat and say it again.

This time, trying to sound like I know what I'm doing. "I'll go."

Nate's dark blue eyes collide with mine. "Come on up!"

The students' eyes stay pinned on me while I shove past them and make my way closer to the gate.

Nate strides up beside me. "Stay calm and walk in slowly. Your match will find you." He opens the gate and lets me pass. "And good luck, Rosa…" He whispers before closing the gate behind me.

I whip my head around, and the corner of his full lips twitch upward, his eyes full of amusement. Heat rises to my cheeks, and I force my attention back onto the many Pegasus around me.

I take them all in. Focusing on every color, height, and personality. Some are more muscular and look ready for war; others are slender and appear fast as a whip. This is impossible to make a choice, but perhaps that's the reason they get to choose you.

I walk slowly and pass through the first section of the field, holding my arms close to my sides. What am I supposed to do?

A small sandy-colored one starts towards me but stops and continues to eat the grass. Nope. I pass by a large reddish-brown Pegasus and stop. You maybe?

I take a deep breath and turn towards the brown-winged creature. It lifts its head and takes me in before walking away.

It's okay—I can do this.

Keeping my pace slow, I walk to the end of the pasture. Not a single one moves in my direction. I pause for a long moment. Maybe there won't be a match for me because I'm just not cut out for this place. I sigh, and when a long white nose slides over my shoulder, I freeze. Breathe.

I pet the soft nose that's now resting on me. This is strangely familiar. Breathing in, I gently turn around. "Wait, Stardust?"

My eyes meet large green ones, and when I brush at the hair between her eyes, a crescent moon reveals itself.
"I should have known it would be you." I whisper, turning slowly to look back at the gate.

Okay, now what?

The group moves closer to the fence to get a better look at us. I start toward the students and look over my shoulder at Stardust, who is now following behind me. A smile tugs at my lips as we make our way back to the fence.

Nate smirks, opening the gate to let me through just as Henry approaches us. "I figured you two would be together, after that little mare showed a liking to you yesterday."

I smile at Henry and nod. "Yeah? She's great."
Nate turns to the group of excited students, all now ready to be paired up. "Who's up next?" He calls out.

I watch as each of the eight remaining applicants and ten students find their Pegasus. Tess matches to a small sandy-colored gelding.

A slim girl with auburn hair makes her way back to the gate. Not matched. She didn't get chosen by any of them. A sob escapes her lips, and she pushes past the students, darting back to the academy.

That was harsh. How is that fair?

An hour passes just as the last student gets paired with their Pegasus. Nate and I exchange brief glances during, creating an electric pull that's wildly confusing. Why didn't he tell me he was the assistant instructor here?

Seeing his features in the daylight has me completely distracted, and I need to stop staring. But I wouldn't have acted like that last night if I'd known who he was...

Henry calls the group to his attention. "Unfortunately, for those of you who are unpaired today, if you haven't already, you shall take your leave."

He pauses. "For the rest of you, I will divide this group into two, as I mentioned earlier. The first-year students will primarily be under my supervision. My assistant, Nate, will oversee the scholarship applicants as they compete. Now, remember the name of the Pegasus you paired with because after lunch you will all be meeting back in the stables."

The group stands silent as if waiting for further instructions. Nate speaks up. "You're dismissed. Meet in the stables after lunch!"

Jamie elbows me and turns towards the main building. "Come on, let's go." She breathes.

She wants me to go with her? What's going on? I follow and catch up with her. "Okay, wait up!"

She elbows me again. I huff, rubbing my arm. "Ouch—stop it!" I turn my head to look over my shoulder, and Nate's eyes lock into mine. I smile and look away.

She laughs dryly. "So, what was up with you and instructor Nate?" She prods.

Heat fills my cheeks. "W-what?"

Her brows shoot up. "Exactly, he couldn't keep his eyes off

you. And you can't seem to resist his attention. You don't wanna get involved with an instructor, even if he's just the assistant."

I can only shrug. "That's not true! He was not! And technically he's an assistant trainer, and probably a third or fourth-year student. He looks only a couple of years older than us…"

She glances back at the instructors before meeting my gaze. "Yeah, he just graduated. And for someone who isn't interested, you seem to make a lot of excuses!" She teases.

This time I elbowed her. "Hey…"

She lets out a huff of annoyance. "Whatever! Let's just go to lunch."

✧
✧ ✧

Chapter 10

Overly enthusiastic students fill the stables. Today apparently is the simple day of physical training, to bond with the Pegasus you paired with.

Stardust stands in front of me with her halter attached to two cross-ties that are hooked up on either side of the aisle.

Nate strides closer to us and holds up a container full to the brim. "What's all this?" I ask.

He smiles. "It's now your grooming kit for Stardust. As part of your bonding exercise, you must take care of her."

"I thought we were supposed to just fly and compete against each other?"

He sighs softly. "This is stage one. Before the two of you fly anywhere, you need to build some trust."

I tuck a strand of loose hair behind my ear. "Build trust?"

"Mmhm." His lips twitch, like he is withholding a smile. "It is a necessary thing when you are flailing around in the sky learning to fly as a team. You need to trust each other."

Is he mocking me? I can't get a read on him. "Okay, well. How do I do that?"

His dark blue eyes flicker from the container to my eyes again, and he hands me a brush. "Start with this. She needs to know that you want to have a genuine bond. Before the two of you even leave the ground."

I take the brush and the container. His calloused hand brushes over mine for a second, and I flinch at the contact. I give him a shy smile. Maybe he didn't notice me flinching?

Who am I kidding…he totally saw that. "Thanks. For the grooming kit." I mutter.

He nods, and the moment his intense blue eyes shift from mine to help the other applicants, I become acutely conscious of how little attention I pay to anything else when he's this close. I look down the aisle and spot Jamie brushing her chestnut gelding.

The words that I'm learning feel foreign to my tongue, but it's surprisingly fun to practice them. Aidan strides down the aisle and waves in my direction. His toothy smile and excitement to see me has me stifling a bubble of laughter. I wave back as he approaches.

"Wow, you got paired with Stardust! Sorry, I missed all the action! I was getting everything set up here."

"Oh, it's alright." I hold up the container. "So how should

I go about this, the best way?"

He grins. "I'll show you!"

I giggle at his enthusiasm. "I was hoping you'd say that."

He pulls out each brush and item, explaining how to groom and pick out her hooves. "This is a hoof pick, a soft brush, comb for her mane and tail." He continues.

I nod along, trying to commit to memorizing each word. "Okay, I think I've got it. Thanks, Aidan."

He brushes his hands together. "Of course. I've gotta finish mucking out the stalls. Catch you later!"

I smirk at the boy who flails his arm in a cheery wave as he strides back down the aisle. He must be the happiest person I've ever met. I shake my head and turn back to Stardust and start brushing long strokes on the side of her neck. I grab out each item and practice using them, just like Aidan explained.

As I bend down to clean her hoof, Stardust shifts sideways, out of reach. I sigh and look up at the white mare. "Hey—now. Hold still, please."

I huff in frustration as I go for her hoof again. She steps even further away.

Nate appears on her other side and pushes a hand onto her hindquarters. Stardust steps back over to me, clearly understanding his instructions.

I stare in amazement. "H—how did you just do that?"

He smiles before coming around to my side. "It's simple, really. They respond to pressure and body language. Let's just say that the way you approach her and pick up her leg matters."

Interesting. It's easier said than done, though. "Do you mind showing me?" I meet his eyes.

The corner of his mouth turns up. "That's what I'm here for." He clears his throat and continues. "So, instead of approaching her head-on, bring your body sideways up against hers. Like this."

He walks closer to her and pats her neck before turning and bringing his body sideways tight up against her front leg, now bending over facing her hind end. "You see, before you even ask her to bring her leg up, you need to show her through your body language what you are asking of her as well."

I nod and look down at my muddy boots. "There is a lot more to this than just jumping on their backs, huh?"

He chuckles at that. "Yes. Now, watch." Nate bends down while brushing her leg with his hand, and Stardust lets him have it. "See? And when you are cleaning out her hooves, pick in this direction." He motions with his fingers before standing up straight.

I can do this. "Got it, thanks."

"No problem." He turns to leave, and his shoulder brushes mine as he passes.

I suck in a quiet breath and look back at Stardust. Why does his nearness do this to me? I shove that down and get to practicing what he just showed.

I need to focus…

* * *

After an hour of grooming and sneaking in quick conversations with Jamie, Nate makes his way to the middle of the aisle and stands on a wooden trunk outside of a stall.

He calls the students to his attention. "This first week of training will comprise fitness exercises, bonding with your Pegasus, and equine classes. In week two we will begin riding and flight training in the covered arena, and at the end of week three, there will be the first trial race—"

A guy standing with a grey Pegasus scoffs. "Shouldn't we just compete already and get it over with? When will the first trial race be?" He snorts.

Nate turns his attention to the guy with short brown hair, who has rudely interrupted. "What is your name?" He commands.

The boy with green eyes stands up straighter, and a smirk forms on his thin lips. "James Harlo."

Nate's jaw twitches. "Well, James. The team will receive more information during the second week of training."
He turns his attention back to the group. "The first trial race will have ten applicants, if everything goes according to plan. Depending on your performance in training, leadership will make cuts based on your weekly rankings. And the first two practice races will determine which three of you will make it to the final competition to win the scholarship deal."

I swallow hard. There are only three spots left for the last race? A couple of shouts erupt from the students.

"No one said anything about cuts being made before the first race even starts!" James's sharp and nasally voice rings out.

Oh boy, here we go…

Nate lifts a hand in the air. "Quiet! Those are the rules. Take it or leave it." He runs a hand through his short, raven hair. "Now, finish up here at your leisure and put your Pegasus in its assigned stall when you're done. After dinner, you have free time." He sighs. "Tomorrow, the fitness aspect of training begins bright and early in the gym."

He steps off the trunk, and I let my eyes linger on him as he strides out of the stables.

Chapter 11

The sun sets over the mountains from my dorm room window. Jamie sits on her bed, listening to music and ignoring me, as per her typical behavior. I turn and grab my phone off my dresser and call home.

My heart quickens at the ring.

"Hello?" Grandma June's soft voice calls out.

I sit on my bed and cross my legs. "Hey, Grandma. It's Rosa. I'm calling from the academy."

My chest tightens. This is the longest I've been away from her since the accident.

After a long moment, she replies. "My Rosa! How are you, dear?"

The excitement in her voice has me holding back tears, and I fill her in on everything that has happened in the past few days. When she yawns and says that Nurse Meyers is gonna help get her to bed, we say our goodbyes and hang up.

I glance back up at Jamie, who now sits at the edge of her bed. A frown line forms between her dark eyebrows, her headphones draping around her neck. "Yeah, I definitely don't have someone at home who cares for me like that."

I turn my body to face her. "I'm sorry—want to talk about it?"

She half-laughs, half-scoffs. "Not much to tell. My parents are workaholics, and my older brother is in law school. This is my one shot at proving myself. The irony is that I know I won't meet my parents' expectations even if I succeed here."

That's harsh. How could her parents not be proud of her for making it?

I slide to the edge of my bed. "We don't have to talk if you don't want to. But if you want, I'm here. That's what roommates are for, right?"

She laughs dryly. "What planet are you from? You spend way too much time with your grandmother; it shows."

The pain underneath her sarcasm is startling, and in this moment I realize that her gruffness must be an act.

I sigh and look down at my hands, tears pricking my eyes. "You say that like it's a bad thing…"

Jamie slides off her bed. "Sorry, Rosa. I didn't mean it like that."

I keep my gaze on my hands. "It's alright, really. But you may as well know since you shared with me…"

She might as well know, right?

Sighing, I look up at her dark-lined eyes. "Five years ago, my mom and I were in a car accident. I was in the backseat; my mom died on impact. I've been with my grandma ever since."

Jamie stiffens at my words. "I didn't—I'm so sorry."

She breaks eye contact, avoiding my sorrowful gaze. "I wouldn't have gone on complaining about my parents if I'd known…"

I give her a small smile. "It's okay, you didn't know. There's a lot we don't know about each other, I guess."

She looks up, a mischievous smile spreading across her lips. "I have an idea…"

"And what might that be? I'm not going to any cliff parties, just so you know."

She waves her hand at me. "It's something better, trust me!"

What has gotten into her? I laugh. "I'm not sure I do trust you!"

She grabs my arm and forces me out the door. "Where are we going?" I grumble.

She smiles widely. "Oh, come on! We are just getting ice cream."

A bubble of laughter escapes us both, and I can't help but

think this intimidating girl might somehow turn into my closest friend here.

* * *

The image of my mom fades as I fling my eyes open and clutch at my chest. Just a dream. Just a dream. I slide out of bed. Jamie shifts in hers, sound asleep.

I have to get out.

Moonlight creeps in through the curtain of the window, and I slip on my athletic wear and sneak out the door. The cool breeze on my face and the stillness of the starry night already calms my racing heart as I make my way down the path towards the stable.

A whinny sounds to my left as I pass by the long pastures, and I jump, clutching my chest. Stardust's frame and white coat become visible as she approaches the fence.

"What are you doing out, girl? I thought you stayed in the barn at night." I whisper into the darkness.

She steps closer to the fence to greet me, and I close the distance. Her soft, warm nose nestles into my shoulder.

"Good to see you, too."

A smile spreads across my lips. I could get used to this, and I can't decide if that terrifies me or excites me. We stand for a few moments, and I stroke my fingers over her long face and jawline. She pulls away and turns her body, stepping closer to the fence.

"What are you—"

She adjusts her wings at her side and presses her body tight against the wooden posts. Wait, she wants me to ride her?

"I don't think that's such a good idea."

Stardust whinnies and stomps her hoof. I grab the top of the fence and hoist myself up. "Fine...okay!"

Here goes nothing...

I reach forward and grasp her coarse mane in my hands. Stardust stands still as I swing my leg over the fence and hop up on her back. This is how they do it in old westerns, right? Minus the large wingspan... I adjust my legs to sit behind her large white wings, a shaky breath escaping me.

The heat of her body warms my legs as I hold them tightly around her. "Okay, girl. Now what?" I mumble.

She abruptly starts forward, and my whole body tightens around her. I take a deep breath and try to relax as she walks us across the moonlit field. Each step forward feels like magic. Every muscle in my core and legs starts engaging. So, this is the reason there's a ton of physical training. We walk around for a while, and I breathe in the deep mountain air. I let my body sway and find the rhythm of her movements, taking it all in.

I brush her neck and let her powerful wings hold me in place. That is until she stretches them out and flaps once before bringing them back to her side, my leg muscles flinching at the movement. What is she doing?

There's no way she'd…

"Don't you dare!" I whisper harshly.

Stardust takes off into a gallop, and my heart lurches. I grip her neck and tighten my legs around her.

This is it—I'm going to die. So much for the competition! I hear myself squeal. After a moment, we are airborne.

Chapter 12

I hold my breath as her vast wingspan rises and falls, sending my stomach into chaos. When Stardust levels out to a smoother rhythm, I open my eyes and adjust my body that's still clung to her long neck with a death grip. I slowly lean further from her frame and dare to straighten my back.

My heart hammers in my chest, and the wind whips at my face, sending my loose hair into disarray. The stars fan out like a maze around me, and I let out the breath I was holding. Don't look down. Just don't look down.

The instructors are gonna kill me…that is if I don't fall to my death first.

Stardust tilts to the left, and my muscles tighten with the movement. My hips slide, and I feel myself slipping. A weight drops into the pit of my stomach. Crap.

My forearms burn with fatigue as I grip tighter and pull myself closer to her again. The flutter of another set of wings sounds behind me. What is going on?

I lean forward, bringing my face closer to her neck, and chance a glance behind me. A large black Pegasus and rider follow us. Shoot. I'm in deep trouble now…this is not good. The rider disappears below us and returns into view ahead of us.

I squint my eyes and try to make out the figure. Short, dark hair, and a lean build. Confident movements. Nate? Shoot! Why'd it have to be him? Why does that make it even worse?

He motions with his arm to follow, and Stardust sets into a smooth rhythm behind them as we begin our descent. My stomach flips, and I close my eyes before we hit the ground.

I brace for the harsh impact, but it doesn't come.

We land gracefully in the lush field, and Nate's voice calls out next to me. "What were you thinking?! You could've fallen!" He pants.

I open my eyes and adjust my body as Stardust brings her wings together, tucking them at her side.

My chest heaves, the adrenaline of what just happened settling in, and I run a hand over my tangled hair. I didn't fall—I made it. How did I not just fall to my death?

I let my eyes focus on the silhouette of the Pegasus and rider.

Nate rides closer and clears his throat. "Hello? What in the world were you thinking, Rosa?" Frustration fills his tone, and I shudder.

"I—uh. She was just walking and before I knew what was happening, we were in the air—" I say, breathless.

A groan mixed with subtle laughter fills the darkness between us. "It's a miracle you didn't fall and die—you could lose your place in the competition because of this."

Would he rat me out like that? I guess so, it's his job. "Are you gonna say anything?"

There's a long pause before he answers. "Haven't decided that yet. Your little nighttime escapades should not entail hopping on a Pegasus when you don't know how to fly."

"I wasn't planning on riding her—it just kind of happened." I can't tell if he's mad at me or amazed…

Nate just stares at me. "Well, don't make it a habit if you wanna make it to the second week of training. It sort of requires staying alive…" He says.

A soft giggle escapes me, and I brush my hand over Stardust's soft neck. "I'll try to keep my nighttime escapades to a minimum. But thanks for the save up there."

They stride closer. "You're welcome. Why do you come out here at this hour, anyway? You don't strike me as the late-night party girl."

He turns his Pegasus away and I straighten, tightening my grip on her mane as Stardust strides forward alongside them. "I have my reasons. Like I said, I just needed some air. And it's because I'm not that girl."

"Well, you definitely got some of that fresh air!" He chuckles.

I nearly snort and stifle a bubble of laughter. He thinks he's so funny… Okay, maybe he is. Just a little.

We ride next to each other in silence, and I lift my head once more to the starlit sky.

His voice softens. "So, you aren't gonna tell me why you so desperately needed some air?"

I look over at his face cast in darkness and moonlit shadows. "I don't even know you. What about you, hmm? Why are you strolling around at this hour?"

He strokes the mane of his Pegasus. "I don't know, maybe because a new girl seems to want to put her life in danger."

What a punk! I laugh dryly. "Hilarious! I was doing just fine, thank you very much." I run a hand through my loose hair. "So, how long have you been an instructor?" I ask.

He sighs. "You're avoiding my first question…"

I grin, though in this darkness it doesn't matter. "And you're being nosy…"

He shakes his head. "Alright, fair answer. I guess I'll find out—eventually."

I giggle. "I guess you will…or not."

We approach the stable, and he dismounts. I slide off her back and find my footing in the grass, my legs tired and wobbly. We stand face to face, perhaps a little too close in the dark. Butterflies dance in my stomach as I step back, hating that his closeness affects me like this. Yet this is not how I imagined this night would go—in a good way.

I should get going. "It's late; I should get back to my room."

He steps back, resting an arm on his Pegasus. "Yeah. I'll take care of them, you can go."

He doesn't sound very enthusiastic about that. Maybe he wants to keep talking?

"Are you sure?" I breathe.

He smiles down at me. "Mmhm. Goodnight, Rosa."

Well, if he's sure. "Thank you for not saying anything about this. Goodnight, Nate." I turn and start across the pasture and back up to my dorm room.

Chapter 13

My lungs burn. I gasp for air, willing my legs to keep running. Is all this really necessary?

Jamie passes to my left as I turn the corner of the track in the gym, completing my last lap. I suck in a shallow breath and adjust the black tank top that now clings to my sweaty frame.

Tess strides by, her nose lifting in disgust. "Dang. You're out of shape!" She laughs and calls to her friend, who approaches her side. "Lila, don't you think the new girl reeks of—"

Before she can finish her insult, I turn away and start towards the group of applicants mixed with first and second years. I won't let her have the satisfaction of her insult reaching my ears.

She's just plain mean; I don't care what she thinks.

They all sit near the fitness equipment in the center of the gym after completing their laps. I stride closer, and Jamie tosses me a water bottle. "You look how I feel! Only a few months without training and it's kicking my butt."

She glances behind me then meets my gaze again. "Don't worry about Tess. It's only her first year. But she acts like a brat because she practically grew up here."

"Yeah, a butt-kicking to say the least! I have no training under my belt. As for Tess, yeah, I'm trying not to let her get to me."

I sit beside her and lean back on my palms. "Lunch is sounding pretty good right about now…"

I brush a sticky strand of hair from my forehead before the group turns their attention to Nate approaching.

"Five minute break! Weight training will begin shortly." His gaze sweeps across the group before his eyes meet mine.

Nate's eyes linger on me, and for a heart-stopping moment, I'm caught in his stare before he turns and heads back to the office beside the gym, the viewing window reflecting the fluorescent lights.

Henry peers through the glass before turning his back to the group and striking up a conversation with him. I peel my eyes away, back to my newfound friend.

Jamie snorts. "Yes, Sir!"

I giggle and shake my head at her. "Careful he doesn't

hear you—" I mutter.

Her dark-lined eyes meet mine, and she smiles. "Oh, stop being such a goody two-shoes. Aren't you trying to get his attention?" She teases.

I give her a shove. "Not like that, I'm not!" I take a long sip of water. "Anyway, I've been meaning to ask, what is it like being on the team?"

"A ton of work! Don't get me wrong, it's amazing. But I spent the whole first year training my butt off to get put on the traveling team to compete around the world."

That's incredible. "Wow, I didn't realize. There are teams around the world?"

"Yup, crazy, I know. Come this Spring, I'll be packing for Europe for my first big leagues competition, the Flyers Cup—" Her words trail off when Henry and Nate close in on the group.

The chatter around us ceases, all eyes darting to him.

Henry clasps his hands behind his back. "Both first and second years will start on the equipment. Each applicant will also rotate through the system."

Nate steps forward. "The goal is to condition legs, core, and arms. Second-years help the newcomers as they go. If anyone has a question, just ask. Now, get to work!"

* * *

Over an hour has passed by the time everyone is done with rotations. My legs wobble like jelly as we all make our way to the cafeteria and sit down.

"I don't think my muscles could feel worse." I grumble, fixing my ponytail.

Jamie shifts in her seat beside me, rubbing her shoulder. "Just wait—it gets better." She sighs. "Thankfully, it's equine behavior class and grooming time this afternoon."

I half sigh, half laugh. "Sitting in a classroom sounds pretty good right now…I never thought I'd be saying that."

Jamie chuckles dryly. "Welcome to EFA!"

Chapter 14

The first week flew by, filled with weight training, bonding with Stardust, and classes. Trying to avoid Tess Fletcher is proving to be difficult, and so is sneaking out for air at night unnoticed.

My mind wanders to the night I rode Stardust. But also deep blue eyes and raven hair. Nate. When I sneak glances during training, nine times out of ten our eyes meet, my heart thunders, and I turn away.

I sigh, shaking my head. He is the last thing I need to me thinking of, especially with flight training tomorrow. He must know that, too.

Every muscle in my body aches as I sit up straight in the cushioned chair of the small library. Yawning deeply, I try my hardest to focus on the words before me. Now that it's past nine, the room is eerily quiet, and it's almost impossible to keep going. After re-reading the same sentence again and again, I shut the book about Pegasus. I can't believe that tomorrow we get to fly…

I leave the library and pass several students on my way to my dorm room. Navigating the halls has become easier, and I take the stairs two at a time, veering to the right.

When I open the door, I find Jamie sitting cross-legged on her bed. She sighs in annoyance. "There you are. I've been waiting to get going."

Guilt settles in the pit of my stomach. "Sorry—I lost track of time and completely forgot." I say briskly.

Jamie straightens her back, eyebrows raising. "You agreed to go with me! We are gonna miss all the fun. Now hurry!"

I sigh at her persistence. "Ok—ok! After this, though, you've gotta stop nagging me to go with you. Deal?"

"Deal." She shakes her head triumphantly. "But change your outfit…you can't wear training clothes."

I raise my brow, glancing down at my sweats and t-shirt. "Why can't I wear this?"

She plops off her bed. "Ah…because it's a party. Come on, haven't you been to a party before?"

I scratch my neck, heat rising to my cheeks. "Actually, no. I haven't. Most of my high school years, I took care of my grandma and worked after school. Left little time for parties."

"Oh." She goes to my dresser and starts fumbling through my clothes. "Well, I know just how to help."

Her bluntness continues to catch me off guard, and I shake my head as Jamie hurls dark skinny jeans at me, then strides to her dresser.

"Is all this really necessary?" I prod.

"Yes." Jamie pulls out a fitted burgundy long-sleeve and tosses it to me before turning to her mirror to apply a cherry-red lip gloss, plumping her lips.

I sigh loudly in hopes she realizes how ridiculous I find this party stuff. I quickly change my clothes and take out my ponytail, letting my long hair fall over my shoulders.

"Better?" I ask.

She twists around and throws her lip gloss at me. "The final touch! Let's go!"

I catch it and smudge some on. "Okay—I'm as ready as I'll ever be." I lace up my boots and follow her out the door, a knot twisting in my stomach. "We aren't gonna be out super late, right?"

She smiles and grabs my arm. "Just trust me, okay?"

I'm still not so sure about this. "Fine!" I mumble as we descend the stairs.

* * *

Twenty minutes later, I trudge alongside Jamie down a worn-down path in the woods behind the school. She flicks her flashlight to the right, revealing stone-like steps descending into darkness above.

I cautiously watch my step as my foot catches on a large tree root. "This is where the party is?" I ask.

She just chuckles. "Oh my gosh, can you please have a little patience! You'll see soon enough!"

We climb the sketchy staircase, and after a few minutes, music echoes through the trees. My heart quickens when campfire smoke fills my nose as we reach the top. The huge stone platform appears, and a cave's half-dome hangs above.

Around fires, at least a dozen or two students are sitting and standing in groups, chatting. The opposite end looks dark, and only a couple of students stand close to the edge.

The cliff…?

I follow Jamie as she approaches the closest bonfire. She waves to them, taking a seat and motions for me to follow suit. "Hey, guys. This is Rosa. She's competing for the scholarship," she says.

All eyes flick to me, and I wave shyly. "Hi…"

I feel so stupid just standing here. This is ridiculous. I squint and glance around the fire as names spew out around me.

Jasper, Eddy, Victoria.

Each student emanates a certain air of confidence. They've gotta be second or third-year students. I take in the group of Jamie's friends in the firelight, dressed in dark colors, and sit down on the rough blanket beside her. I try to drown out the music and focus on the conversations developing around me.

They go on trading stories of how they first paired with their Pegasus, first classes, and silly crushes. Footsteps fall close behind me, and before I know it, a guy plops down beside me, and I stiffen. What does he think he's doing..?

He crosses his legs and flashes me a flirtatious grin. "Hey, I'm James. I've seen you around."

His tone is smooth and well-practiced. I take in his short brown hair, sharp nose, and thin lips. He's the one who challenged Nate…

I try my best to give a polite smile. "Hi, I'm Rosa."

He puffs out his chest, making his muscles embarrassingly obvious. "Can I get you a drink?"

I tilt my head down. "Uh—no. But thanks."

Turning my attention back to Jamie, I try to give him the

hint that I'm not interested. Hopefully, he'll figure it out sooner than later…if he's smart.

He clears his throat, voice dropping low. "So, you wanna take a walk…?"

I turn my head and catch his gaze just in time to see his eyes trail up and down my body. I'm not going anywhere with this creep. Absolutely not.

"With you? No, I'll be staying right here." I say, full of confidence in my decision to stay. Maybe I'm being too rude? I give him a polite smile.

Jamie shifts beside me. "Hey, dude! Leave her alone; she's obviously not interested."

I'm glad Jamie is so direct, and I tell myself to thank her later. James scratches his jawline, embarrassment rising in his cheeks. Like a light switch, his expression changes from flirtatious to hard anger in seconds.

Woah, this guy's got issues…

He stands abruptly and makes his way to another fire, shoving anyone in his way. I shake my head, glad I listened to my gut.

A high-pitched shriek fills my ears, and I whip my head around again, just in time to see a girl plummeting to the stone floor. A sickening crack sounds, cutting through the music. James steps away, unbothered by the destruction he has caused. The girl cries out in pain and clutches her arm.

"I think—it's broken!" A sob escapes her lips.

Jamie and I glance at James, who seems to be the one who pushed the poor girl. "Yikes. They'll probably disqualify her—they have to take her to the infirmary." My friend whispers.

I stand up and observe her companions helping her to her feet, and they then move towards the path that leads back to the academy.

A moment later, a figure appears. "Alright, the party's over!" Nate's authoritative voice carries over the music, and his flashlight blinds people as he rotates it around the cliff face.

Jamie and her friends rise to their feet next to me. People rush to silence the music and extinguish the flames before going around him to the stairs. Nate strides closer to us.

"Ms. Lynch, may I have a word?"

What could he possibly want? I turn my head to face Jamie. She eyes me wearily in question.

I nod and try to reassure her. "It's okay. I'll meet up with you in the dorm."

She nods before looping her arm in Jasper's, and they all take off down the path along with the others. Nate closes the distance between us.

"Seems to me you may be a party girl after all," he says, a hint of sarcasm in his tone.

I shake my head. "No, my friend Jamie has been harassing me to come. So I told her that if I came tonight, then she had to let it go after this."

I stand my ground, though I don't know why his assumptions bother me so much. Why do I care so much about what he thinks of me?

His eyes lock into mine. "I see. So, what happened?" I tuck a strand of hair behind my ear, the smell of smoke lingering in my nose as I glance at the dying embers of the fire. "Over there, a girl fell. Well, I think James pushed her, I can't prove it completely. She probably broke her arm."

He pauses for a long moment. "Mmm, I had a feeling James was becoming a problem. But can you prove it was him?"

I sigh in frustration. "It's dark. I didn't see him physically push her, but he was shoving people and storming away after he—"

He cuts in. "After he what...?"

I clear my throat. "He just got mad. I–ahh, might've turned him down or something like that."

He stifles a laugh. "Interesting..."

What's his deal? "It's not funny! The guy is a jerk."

Nate stiffens. "Yeah, I know. He is proving to be a loose cannon. Since tomorrow is the first day of flight training, they will post the first rankings, so you should keep your distance. I have heard of applicants who go to great lengths to keep their spot."

I nod and rub my arms, trying to ward off the shivers without the warmth of the fire. "What will happen to the injured girl? She won't be able to race for the scholarship?"

He sighs. "Breaking her arm will disqualify her from the competition."

That's ridiculous; it wasn't even her fault. "How is that fair?" I challenge him.

We are both silent for a moment before he glances away into the darkness. "It's not always fair. However, those are the rules here," he says.

I stare at the tiny flames nearby, which are fading fast.

He steps closer, lowering his voice. "Come on, I'll make sure you get back okay."

I press my lips together, refraining from saying more, and turn back to meet his dark blue eyes. "Okay—yeah. Thank you." I mutter.

He turns onto the path, his flashlight illuminating the way.

I walk next to him, and he gently nudges my shoulder.

"I'm thinking perhaps you are trouble after all, legacy." He teases.

Chapter 15

My heartbeat quickens as I set the grooming kit on the ground in front of the stall and zip my uniform further up my neck. Aidan calls out from a nearby stall he's been cleaning out for the last several minutes. "Good luck, Rosa!" He sings songs.

A smile spreads across my lips. "Thanks!"

I unlatch the cross-ties from Stardust's halter in the aisle and gently pull on the reins. "Come on, girl."

Anticipation builds in my gut as I follow the line of applicants and Pegasus now filing out of the stables. My long ponytail swings across my back with each step. Today, I put my life on the line. Today...I fly.

Jamie strides up as we step out of the barn. "Are you ready?"

"If terrified is what you call ready, then, sure. Are you coming to see me ride?" I ask.

She places her hands on her hips. "Wish I could. I've

gotta get back to the gym for more leg and core training."

"Fun, fun..." I say, dripping with sarcasm.

She turns with a smile. "Remember, don't fall off and die!"

I shake my head at her. "Nice! Thanks!"

Moving in line down the path, I wait my turn to lead Stardust into the training dome. I run a hand over her soft neck and glance at the few students behind me, standing with their Pegasus. James catches my glance, and if his eyes could shoot daggers, I'd be dead right now.

A shiver runs down my spine, and I turn my head as the line moves forward. We each pass through a large, garage-like door into the arena. Soft, sandy dirt meets my feet, and I wiggle my toes in my new boots. Henry and Nate stand in the middle of the arena, directing each pair who enters to a specific side. Stardust and I stride closer to them, and Nate instructs us to the right side of the arena.

The enormous domed roof looms over us, and I crane my neck to get a better look. It's like nothing I've ever seen before. I follow suit and line up next to each pair of applicants and watch the rest of the students file in and get separated. The applicants are eerily quiet as we wait in anticipation of what happens next.

Stardust nudges closer, and I run my fingers through her

snow-white mane.

As the last pair falls into line, Nate walks over to us, facing the group. "Congratulations, applicants. You've made it to the second week of training." He crosses his arms over his chest and stares down the line. "We will now determine your score via rankings, starting with today's training. At the end of today, these judges—"

He points up to a viewing box built high into the side of the dome. "Over the two weeks leading up to the first trial race, they will watch each of you train and determine your score. Our safety protocol could disqualify the applicant with the lowest ranking."

Lila gasps next to Tess and me, and I bite my tongue to hold back my questions.

Now is not the time. Not right now.

Nate meets my gaze, and a sudden wave of warmth floods his eyes before his features settle back into the familiar, composed instructor.

He bends down and grasps a long black item from a box at his feet and holds it up. "This girth has two leg straps, made up of a unique design of elastic and paracord. This helps you keep a general balance, but it will not inhibit your body from giving the correct signals. Though the bands will not hold most of your body's full weight, that is why leg and core training are important."

His eyes narrow down the line of applicants. "You will be in this covered training arena this week. There will be flight training twice a day, every day. Next week we will move your training outside to a different location. Now, who wants to put the girth on their Pegasus first?"

Tess all but leaps and throws her hand in the air. "Me! I'll do it!" She flashes him a flirtatious smile as he approaches her.

An uneasy feeling settles in my gut as I watch them.

Nate hands her the girth and gives a quick example of how to put it on her gelding. Tess nods and slides the girth on around her sandy-colored Pegasus, cinching it tight just behind its wings.

Nate pivots, his eyes examining down the line. "You need to wait a few minutes to re-tighten the girth after the initial cinch. They adjust to it, and it needs to be fitted to prevent it from sliding around," he says.

The applicants nod, absorbing the instructions. I feel myself doing the same. Jame's heavy gaze lingers on me, and I try my best to ignore him.

Nate walks back to the box and grabs the rest of the girths, handing them out to each of us. "Get to work." He instructs.

The girth is soft but firm as I wrap it around Stardust's back behind her wings. I tighten the cinch only a couple of notches like Tess did, then watch as Nate paces the length of the line, examining each applicant's work.

His eyes meet mine, and I swear I see a faint smile on his lips when he nods his approval, but it vanishes as he passes, breaking our contact. Ten minutes later, each applicant has successfully placed the girths on.

Chapter 16

Nate stops again, addressing the applicants. "Every Pegasus responds to pressure in their own way. That's why it's important to learn their body language. This may feel foreign to you, but when you apply hip pressure on the right, their natural escape from the pressure will be to move to the left to get away from it. So, your steering will be opposite of what you may have thought."

He goes on. "You will have a simple halter and reins. Again, you will do most of your steering with your body. But when you use your reins, you will use what is called indirect rein and move your leg and hip at the same time as your hands. Like this…"

He walks over to me. "Ms. Lynch, will you help me show them?" He asks, voice even.

Me? I nod and swallow hard. "S-sure." I mumble.

He strides closer and cinches Stardust's girth tighter before he bends down low, lacing his hands together. "Step up." He whispers.

Taking a deep breath, I lift my left boot into his hands.

This is so weird…

With one hand, I grip the reins and with the other her mane while he hoists me up. My hands tremble, but I pull myself together. Though his closeness is irritatingly distracting, I force myself to concentrate and swing my leg over her back, avoiding his eyes.

Stardust adjusts her wings, and I settle in just behind the girth. Nate walks us forward a few feet in front of everyone else and clears his throat. "Watch." He shouts to the group behind us.

Heat rushes to my cheeks as he points out my calves, knees, and hips. Please don't let me look as embarrassed as I feel. His hands find the straps next to my thighs and work fast, showing me how to fasten them around my legs correctly.

I suck in another small breath when he rests a hand on my left knee. "Now, the goal is to move as one. Turn your head to look around to the left and pause there," he says.

What did he just say? Look left?

I breathe out through my nose and turn my head just as he instructs.

Nate's fingers wrap around my knee further. "Watch what

happens to your lower body while you look. Your right leg and knee have naturally pressed in. But see how your left leg and knee have opened up slightly? It gives her a way out."

Did I do it? I examine closer. "Yeah!" I beam.

He takes his warm hand off my knee and wraps his fingers over my hands holding the reins. "You need to use an indirect rein method. The goal is to do what you just told her to do through your body language and hands at the same time."

He shows me again, bringing the right rein against Stardust's neck gently.

He steps back. "Now, you try."

I do just as he instructed and let my lower body move in rhythm with my hands, asking her to do the same exercise. My mare moves out to the left exactly as he explained she would.

A smile spreads across his lips, and my eyes meet his. "Well done." Nate's voice softens. "You will gain more confidence with it as time goes on."

Our little bubble of electricity breaks when he turns back to the line of applicants. How did I forget all eyes were on us? For a moment it was just him and me. I'm just imagining it all, right?

My cheeks burn as I watch him approach the group.

"Tighten your girths and help each other mount up. If you need a mounting block, it is around the edge of the arena. Practice the exercise just showed for at least half an hour. If you need help, call me. After that, we will try takeoff and landing exercises."

Nate answers a couple of applicants' questions, then moves to the edge of the arena, observing the group taking action. I take a deep breath and start the exercise again, asking her to turn now to the right.

Here we go, Stardust. Here we go…

After some time, we move on to take off, practicing every instruction on how to land this exercise safely without being severely injured or even killed.

What feels like hours later, I attempt to take off again. I force my tired legs to grip tighter around Stardust as we take off for the third time, my heart hammering in my chest.

Once again, I adjust my legs and hips to turn her, while fumbling my fingers to move the reins against her neck. We make a wide turn and circle to land, hooves hitting the ground with a thud in the sandy arena. I let out a breath of relief. We did it…

I brush my mare's long, soft neck. "Good job, girl." I whisper as we walk back to the line of applicants.

Nate calls out to the group. "Next!"

Chapter 17

I straighten my stiff back in the wooden chair and peer over the other applicants' heads from the back of the classroom.

Mr. Cato's husky voice beams across the room, and I try to focus my attention back on him, because for the past hour he has taken us through chapter ten of Equine Body Language 101, and I'm struggling to remember each word now.

James wears his usual cocky smirk at the front of the class, peering around, eagerly showing off what facts he has committed to memory this week. Occasionally, Tess will flash me a glare from a distance, and I'll avoid her gaze.

Mr. Cato clears his throat and dismisses the class just as the small bell rings. I swiftly grab my textbooks and rise from my seat, not wanting to spend another second under Tess's glare. A girl sitting next to me with dark brown hair and bright blue eyes darts up and steps in front of me in the small aisle of chairs.

"Hey, wait up. I'm Keira," she smiles. "First year."

I can't help but smile at the abrupt introduction. "Ah–hi. My name's Rosa. I'm competing for the scholarship."

She giggles. "Yeah, I've seen you around. So, some girls are camping out tomorrow night at the cliffs for Jamie's birthday tomorrow. You wanna come?"

I don't think I've ever seen this girl with my friend. "You know, Jamie?"

She waves a hand. "Of course! She said to extend the invitation. Plus, some other applicants wanted to celebrate making it to week three of training the day after."

I nod. "Oh. Yeah, that sounds fun."

Keira beams. "Good. Meet at the cliffs. Tomorrow night at seven o'clock."

* * *

I pivot my feet carefully on the crumbling stone edge of the cliff. The sun sets over the lake beyond, sending perfect golden reflections onto the water before the sun dips below the horizon.

A familiar voice calls out behind me. "Hey—don't get any ideas over there! Come join the party!"

I look over my shoulder and smile at Jamie. "Coming, I was just enjoying the view."

Smoke fills my nose as I pass by the mint green tent Keira picked out and situate myself by the cozy fire the girls have been chatting around for the past hour. A chill runs up my spine, so I pull my black hoodie over my head and let out a sigh.

Jamie laughs across the campfire at something Keira just said before standing to her feet. "So! Who is ready for some truth or dare?!"

Gemma pipes in next to me. "You're the birthday girl! You go first!"

Jamie clasps her hands together, hovering them over her mouth. "Hmm. Eden, truth or dare?"

Eden's cheeks flush red, making her blond hair pop in contrast. "How about truth!"

Jamie smirks. "Hmm—what is your biggest fear?"

Eden's eyes linger on the crackling fire. "Heights..."

Gemma scoffs. "You are afraid of heights and you joined a flight school?!"

Eden giggles. "Yeah, well, that's exactly why I came. Next

person!"

Gemma leans forward. "Ooh—can I pick?"

Jamie nods and sits down, giving Gemma the floor as she stands to her feet. In a matter of seconds, her eyes find mine as she puts a hand on her hip. "Rosa, truth or dare?"

My heart-rate quickens and I swallow hard, hoping my face doesn't reveal my fear. "I guess, truth?"

She flicks her wrist, dramatically waving me off. "That isn't fun at all! Eden just said a truth, now you have to do a dare!"

All the girls cheer in agreement, and Gemma's eyes widen with an idea. "Ah—I have just the thing. Go swim in the lake!"

She points to the edge of the cliff. "Look over there! There's a path down with a rope. I hope you're not scared of heights…"

I shake my head. "No. Absolutely not! How about a different dare?"

The girls groan and raise their complaints. Gemma laughs. "Oh, come on! You big baby!"

My fingers grasp tightly around the rope as I adjust my feet below me. My chest feels like it's about to explode. "This is so stupid." I breathe out.

I descend lower and lower, climbing down the side of

the cliff. Loose rocks crumble out from beneath my feet, and I anxiously grip the rope tighter. The last rays of the sunset are now slowly fading into a blanket of darkness.

By the time I reach the bottom and let go of the rope to drop a few feet to the shoreline, a full moon peaks through the open night sky. I can't believe I'm actually doing this…

Chapter 18

Sand shifts beneath my feet as I walk closer to the large body of water. Here goes nothing…

I untie my sneakers and pull my hoodie back over my head. A small squeal escapes my lips when my toes meet the cold water.

"We always seem to meet under the stars." A familiar voice calls out from behind me.

I nearly jump out of my skin and whip around to face Nate. "Also, didn't anyone ever tell you not to swim at night by yourself?" He teases.

"Trying to scare me half to death, like usual?" I let out a huff. "And who said I'm alone…you're here, aren't you?"

He chuckles in response. "All true. But really, what are you doing out here at the lake?"

"I could ask you the same." I return his flirtatious grin.

"I'm doing my nightly rounds to check parties at the cliff. A regular RA, ensuring everyone follows the rules. You know, in case anyone jumps or climbs down cliffs in the night…"

A giggle escapes me. "Guilty…"

"So, why go for a swim in the lake at night? I'm all too curious." He asks.

I rest my hands on my hips. "Believe me, it wasn't my bright idea. Jamie and the girls dared me. They are camping out up there." I sigh. "Lucky me…I'm the first crazy dare of the night."

His lips press together as he crosses his muscled arms over his chest. "Well, in that case. By all means, have at it."

He doesn't think I'll do it…

I arch a brow, a wide smile spreading across my lips. "Fine, I will."

I take a step further, letting my feet fully submerge into the calm lakeshore. Crap. This is freezing…

Moonlight now reflects off the water, casting shadows as I turn back to face him. "And—I dare you to join me."

"What makes you think I wanna swim in cold water with you?"

"I don't know. Maybe because you can't seem to stay away from me…"

I gulp at the words that just flew out of my mouth, but Nate just chuckles. "You don't say?" He teases.

"Mmm." I can't help but giggle, taking off into the water at full speed. A shriek escapes me as he barrels into the water after me. I dive under the crisp surface, and chills run up my spine before I reach the top again.

Laughter bubbles up in my chest when I hear his voice. "You're full of surprises, aren't you?" His tone is so soft.

How is this man so different around me? Is this really who he is behind the mask of responsibility?

His face is now before mine, and the closeness makes my heart thunder. I run my hands through my damp hair. "So, I still know very little about you…"

He glides his hands across the surface of the water. "Ditto."

I swallow hard. "Okay. So, what are your parents like?"

He smirks. "Of all the questions, Rosa. That's what you want to know about me?"

"Yeah…" I smile. "And by the way, it's Rosamond."

"Ah, see? Full of surprises, Rosamond. I go by a nickname too."

The coolness of the water sends a shiver up my spine. "Wait. Nate is short for something?"

He runs a hand over his short hair. "Yes. Wanna take a guess?"

I stare at him. "Hmm. Nathan?"

He shakes his head. "Classic guess…but nope. You're close though."

Hmm…

Something brushes against my ankle, and I squeal, panic racing through me as I jump. His arms reach out for me and I cling to him like a lunatic.

"It's okay—it's only a fish." He breathes, his face inches from mine now. "Or a scary flesh-eating monster…" He attempts a spooky voice.

I can't tell what's funnier: him teasing me or the fact that I lost it over a tiny fish. Playfully, I swat at his shoulder to which I'm now clung to. "Not even funny! Nate, let's get out of here!"

He chuckles in my ear. "Just a little funny. And it's Nathaniel, actually."

I study his face in the darkness. "Okay—Nathaniel." I tease.

Chapter 19

He carries me out of the lake and sets me down gently in the sand. "There you go. No more scary monsters." He reassures me sarcastically.

My cheeks flush, and I'm thankful he can't see my face that well in the moonlight. I clear my throat. "So, your parents. What are they like?" I ask.

He sits down beside me, straightening his knees and resting his arms on them. This is the most boyish I have seen him yet, and I can't help but take him in as he speaks.

"Well, nothing too extraordinary. My parents are great, though they have always been supportive. It's just me and my younger sister—so my mom likes to think we're the center of her world or something."

Wow, that's really sweet. "I'd say, that's all extraordinary."

He shrugs, perhaps a little embarrassed. "What about you?"

I sigh. "It's not the fairytale you may have imagined."

He nudges my shoulder. "No family is perfect. But you don't have to tell me if you don't want to. I understand."

I let the silence linger for a moment. "My dad left when I was a baby. Just a year old. Growing up, every birthday candle was just a wish for him to come back to us. One day, I realized…I didn't want him to return after everything he put Mom and me through on our own. I could never forgive him."

I take a deep breath and continue. "He passed away two years ago. Now, I'm not sure what to believe about him. I didn't get the chance to find out for myself…"

Silence fills the space between us again until he places his warm hand on my shoulder. "I'm so sorry. No one deserves that. And—your mom?" he asks, his voice gentle.

"She…" My voice cracks. "S-she's gone too."

"Rosa—"

My words cut him off. "My mom and I were in a car accident, and she didn't make it out. Ever since, I've been with my grandmother. I should not have survived that car accident, but somehow I did, with scars in all forms."

He sighs, leaning closer. "I can't even imagine…I'm so sorry you've had to endure all this."

My voice shakes, and I take a deep breath. "Well, I've got my Grandma June. My goal was to find a nursing program at a college close by so that I could continue taking care of her. She was declining slowly at first but after a couple of years, it wasn't so much her looking after a troubled kid anymore as I learned to take care of her. I had to pick up all the pieces on my own."

He takes a deep breath. "I know there aren't many words to say—you are so strong. You have come so far in life already; it seems like there's nothing you can't do."

"Well, thanks." I offer a small smile before snatching up my sweatshirt and shoes. "I should get back before the girls worry or something."

He nods in agreement as we both rise to stand. "I'll walk you back—just not the way you came down."

I giggle. "Oh, what? You don't want to scale the cliff face in the dark?"

He smirks, stuffing his hands in his pockets. "Come on, Rosamond. I have my RA reputation to uphold."

I smile at the mention of my full name that rolls off his tongue so easily and nudge his shoulder as I pass him. "Ah, yes. I wouldn't want to do anything that would harm your flawless reputation…"

He chuckles. "You're a little trouble-maker!"

Shrugging my shoulders, I sigh. "Mmm—that's debatable."

I watch his lips turn up before I sprint off across the sand.

His laughter trails behind me as he hurries to catch up. Nathaniel is going to be quite a distraction after all…

✦ ✦
✦

Chapter 20

I wander through the large hall after breakfast and make my way to the applicants' ranking list on the bulletin board. Skimming over the names to find mine, I swallow hard. Fifth in the rankings to start this week.

Jamie strides up next to me. "Can you believe it? Your first trial race is this Saturday! Are you excited?"

I shiver. "Mostly terrified!"

Her dark eyes brighten. "Hey—when you make it through, we'll all celebrate at the dance on Sunday!"

I can't help but smile at my odd friend. "I love your confidence in me, but let's not get too far ahead of ourselves."

Jamie clutches her stack of books tighter to her chest. "Fine…once you place in the race, we'll go dress shopping and pick out something killer to catch a certain someone's eye."

I shove her and chuckle. "Don't be ridiculous! There is

nothing crazy going on between us."

She arches her brow. "Yeah, right! I didn't even have to say his name and you're already blushing…"

I gawk at her. "Okay—maybe a little something. I hardly know him though, so you can't tell anyone! They'll think I'm just trying to weasel my way into winning the competition…"

Jamie's brow furrows. "And are you doing that?"

I push her again. "Rude! Of course I'm not!"

"I'm just checking," she laughs. "Let's go fly. Try to keep up!"

* * *

Stardust nuzzles her soft nose closer as I stroke her long face. "Are you ready, girl?" I let out a breath through my nose. "I can't believe we made it to week three."

Tess's high-pitched laugh closes in behind me. "I can't believe you did either! I mean, it's a miracle!"

I take a calming breath before turning to face her. "Tess, what are you trying to prove? I earned my place fair and square." I snap.

Tess's eyes narrow, and she leans closer. "You think you're so—" She abruptly straightens, her words getting cut off when Nathaniel stands up on the trunk and calls the group to his attention.

She scowls and turns to leave. "I'm not done with you…"

I focus my attention back on Nathaniel. "Congrats, you made it to week three of training. You may think you have conquered the art of flying by now, but believe me, you haven't. You need to get that inside your head now. Falling off in the competition at this point of training will cause immediate disqualification. So, I would advise you all to take this seriously. Line up and follow me!"

Each Pegasus and rider file in line behind Nate and leave the stable one by one. He veers onto the path that leads to the lake. What training could we possibly be doing at the lake..?

I rub Stardust's soft neck as we follow in the line of applicants on a worn-down path, the clicking of her hooves falling in rhythm with my steps. We can do this. I can do this. Once we reach the shoreline, we line up and face the lake, waiting for the next instruction.

Nathaniel now paces back and forth in front of us.

"Two pairs at a time will practice flying over the lake and getting used to flying together. The goal is to get to the other side and back in one piece."

James scoffs. "Is this even a race?"

Nathaniel's brows come together as he focuses on him. "Yes, this will affect your rankings, if that is what you're concerned about." He moves on from the usual disruptions. "Now, let's get started. James and Gemma up first!"

We watch as James and Gemma mount and take off on the sandy shore, then up into the sky. Without hesitation, he surges ahead, nearly striking her with his Pegasus's wing. He aggressively takes the lead, and my heart quickens when Gemma slips but adjusts herself just in time before she speeds off behind him.

Moments pass before they make it to the other side of the lake and race back at incredible speed. I hold my breath as they grow closer until they are whipping over our heads, James in the lead. He shouts and carries on in his victory as they turn and slow down, landing back on the sandy shore.

Nathaniel turns to face the group. "Up next, Rosa and Eden!"

I swallow hard and meet his eyes. He gives the smallest of smiles as if he's trying to reassure me, but it's gone in a split second.

Here goes nothing… I turn to Stardust, and before I can ask for help, Nathaniel is already at my side. "Need a hand?"

He already knew I'd need it. "Yeah, thanks." I breathe.

Lacing his fingers together, he hoists me up. I tighten the straps around my thighs, taking a deep breath.

He leans closer. "Just stay focused and keep your balance. You got this."

He pats Stardust's neck before stepping away. Eden's eyes find mine, and she nods her head. I nod back.

We barrel across the sand, the wind whipping at my face, and a rush of excitement fills me to the bone. I adjust my weight and lean forward, my heart hammering in my chest as we take off into the sky.

This is what pure adrenaline feels like…

I whip past Eden and her copper-colored Pegasus at perfect speed to get ahead. "Yes! Stardust, we got this!"

I adjust my hips as we make a sharp turn before racing back towards the shore.

Chapter 21

An ear-splitting shriek comes from behind me, and I turn my head just in time to see Eden falling from her Pegasus, plummeting to the water below.

I turn Stardust instantly and race to reach her in time, but it's too late. Her body slams hard into the lake, and she goes under. I steer Stardust to hover above her as best as I can manage. Eden's blond hair shoots up above the surface, and she coughs up water.

Her eyes frantically find mine above as I call out to her. "Eden! What happened? Are you okay?!"

She coughs again, her voice cracking. "One stupid fall and it's all over!"

"Do you want help?!" I shout over fluttering wings.

She turns and begins swimming back to shore. "No! I'll face it myself!"

I can barely make out her words. A weight falls into my stomach. "I'm so sorry!" I call after her and urge Stardust on.

Climbing into the sky, we continue the flight back to the water's edge and land safely in the sand. Cheers erupt from the row of applicants but I can't shake the dread I feel for Eden as she makes it to shore, her lips quivering. I reach for her, but instantly regret it when she completely dismisses me, shoving past.

My eyes find Nathaniel; his gaze flicks to mine, and a half-smile forms on his lips.

After a second, the instructor in him is called to action. "Eden is officially out of the competition. She will no longer be flying with us. Up next—Liz and Conner!

As Conner and Liz take to the sky, I watch as a few of the applicants attempt to say goodbye to Eden as well, with no success. I can't blame her; she's worked so hard for this.

The race is swiftly won by Conner; his ginger ringlets catching in the breeze as he celebrates.

Nathaniel congratulates him before turning to the rest of the group. "We will finish up with Jessica and Ashley."

Chapter 22

I fall into a steady routine each day of week three of training. The muscles in my legs and core are sore, but I can feel myself getting stronger and more confident in the bond I've formed with Stardust.

Standing against the fence, I brush my hand over her soft white nose, which snuggles my shoulder. "Goodnight, girl. We have a big day tomorrow." I whisper.

Aidan strides through the pasture with a bubbly expression on his face, halter and lead rope in hand. "Time to turn her in," he says.

I smile at the dorky kid and his excitement in everything he seems to do. "Alright, sounds good." I practically hum.

He makes his way over to Stardust and slides her halter on. "Don't worry about the race tomorrow; you two were born for this. I heard a little tip from around the stable hands that the race is not what is to be expected." He shrugs his shoulders. "Whatever that means."

Something that isn't expected?

"Thanks, Aidan. I'll keep that in mind. Hopefully, it's nothing too crazy."

He turns, leading Stardust behind him. "You'll do awesome! Gotta get back to work. See you later, Rosa!"

A smile forms on my lips, and I shake my head. "Bye, Aidan."

I watch the sun vanish behind the distant pines and head back into the main building of the academy. A yawn escapes me, and the thought of curling up in bed has my feet shuffling faster and faster.

I round the hall to the giant staircase and slam into something hard. Someone...

Henry smirks as he pulls my frantic frame off him. "Where are you going in such a hurry?" He asks.

Heat rises into my cheeks. "Sorry, I have a habit of rushing up to my room. I didn't see you."

His face softens as he pushes back his hair. "So, how's the legacy doing?"

I cross my arms. "I guess—I'm as good as I can be. But I moved up to fourth in the rankings this week..."

He smiles. "Yes, you are doing very well. And how is your grandmother doing?"

Why is he asking so many questions? Maybe he's just trying to be nice?

"Oh. To be honest, I'm a little worried. She really didn't sound like herself on the phone yesterday. I think I'm going to call Nurse Meyers and make sure everything is going okay."

He runs a hand over the stubble forming on his face. "How about I contact Nurse Meyers and get some information this evening. Go get some sleep; you look beat. The first race is in the morning, so you need to be focused."

I am exhausted. But something is off…

Either that, or he just really cares about all his applicants like this. "Henry, can I ask you something?"

His eyes grow in intensity at my question. "Sure, go ahead."

Do it. I swallow hard. Just ask him. "Why do you care so much about us?"

He crosses his arms, mimicking my posture. "What do you mean?"

How does he not get this?

"I mean…you didn't have to arrange all this." I wave a hand at my surroundings. "Look after me or my grandma—"

Relief fills his face for a moment. "It would be an injustice if I didn't. Knowing your father, he wouldn't have desired anything different, so I will do everything in my power to take care of you both."

Well, I wasn't expecting that. "Thanks. I know I wouldn't have this piece of my parents if you hadn't followed through." I look to the floor before meeting his gaze once again. "But I still hate my father for never caring about us…"

His brows raise slightly. "Your father was a good friend to me. I'm sure he did what he thought was best."

Tears sting my eyes, and I look away. "How was abandoning his wife and baby for the best? How was a child growing up without a dad for the best?"

I bite the inside of my cheek and look away. He falls silent, and I use that as my opportunity to pass him.

A fragile sigh escapes me, all hope for this conversation fading. "I guess you didn't know him as well as you thought you did." I try to soften my voice. "But you're right. I should get some rest. Goodnight, Henry."

There is a long pause before he calls out after me. "Goodnight, Rosamond."

Chapter 23

Nathaniel's voice echoes over the applicants. "This race will require coordination, teamwork, and communication. It will test your ability to see whether you will be fit to be put on a team in the future."

The aisle fills with anticipation as we wait to see how this first race will unfold. His voice grows louder. "There will be two teams. Two captains. James and Rosa, you will be our captains for today. Choose wisely."

Crap…this must be a mistake.

James rolls his eyes. "How can we pick a team when we don't even know what the race is going to be yet?"

Nathaniel ignores him and addresses the group. "That is precisely the point. After you're done, meet me and your teams behind the stables." He hops off the trunk and strides down the aisle.

Jame's eyes flick to mine. "What will it be?" He scoffs.

I straighten my back, hoping I look more confident than

I feel. "You can choose first."

He narrows his eyes. "Your loss. I'll take Gemma and Ashley. You can have Liz, Conner, and Jessica."

I step closer, lifting my head. "Fine. We have our teams."

"Fine."

His eyes harden before turning his back to me. I take a deep breath as we file out of the stables, each team following behind its leader.

Why did I just agree to becoming a leader?

My eyes catch his gaze, and I take another deep breath. He must think I can do this…

Nathaniel folds his arms across his chest as he waits for the teams to line up. "Listen up! Today we will test your abilities through a game—capture the flag. Afterwards, it will be a race back here at the end of the game."

He steps forward, dragging his boot through the dirt, creating a line. "All of you will race back here the second after the game is over. The last two applicants to cross this line will be eliminated from the competition, no matter their team. Don't be confused; the game is a test of your ability to work on a team. If you cannot execute that team-building exercise, you will never return with the flag or place in time."

I swallow hard. How am I going to be captain of a

team…?

Nathaniel steps forward and grabs two purple flags out of his pocket. His eyes lift to the mountains as he points to our race destination. "There are red boundary markers on the mountain. Failure to respect those barriers will cause the disqualification of your entire team. So, work as a team. Be creative and take action. Captains, grab your flags." He motions two purple flags in the air.

James confidently strides forward and snatches it from his hand. I take mine as well, and when my hand brushes his, our eyes lock, the purple fabric pressing into my palm.

Nathaniel's brows come together as he mutters. "Be creative, just not outside the boundaries—"

James cuts off his next words. "Well, are we going to race already?" He complains.

His eyes flick behind me. "Yes." He clears his throat and straightens. "You will first wear wristbands. The buzzer will sound immediately after you win the game, no matter your location. You will then all race back to this starting point." He grabs wristbands from a box and tosses one to each of us. "Let the race begin!"

My heart beats faster as I secure the band around my wrist and turn around to Liz, Conner, and Jessica.

I swallow hard, their eyes already focusing on me.

Liz steps forward, smiling. "So, what's the plan, Captain?"

Plan. A plan. I need a plan…

I watch as James, Gemma, and Ashley take off towards the mountains, pushing their Pegasus hard. Already taking advantage of the high ground. My gaze shifts and settles on Nathaniel. His eyes briefly meet mine, his lips twitching into a smile.

I snap back into the conversation as Liz's black eyes stay pinned on me. "Hello? You have a plan, right?"

Taking a shaky, I breath through my nose.

Think. Think. You need a plan! I lift the flag in my hand. "Well, let's start with defence and offense. Does anyone have a preference?" I ask.

They all eye each other for a long moment, waiting for my instruction. Nate's words replay in my mind. "Be creative, but just not outside the boundaries."

We need a decoy…we need a distraction.

A smile forms on my lips. "Nobody said we couldn't have a decoy flag…" I say, raising a brow.

Conner's eyes brighten at my words, fueling my confidence. This idea might just work.

I slide off my purple and black zip-up, revealing my fitted black tank. "This purple. It will work as a decoy from a distance in the brush—I will hide it and pretend to guard it. Jessica—you take the real flag."

I press purple fabric into her palm and turn to the others as words spew from my mouth. "Conner and Liz, you're going on offense. Retrieve their flag."

Jessica nods, and the others follow suit.

This is really happening, and I think we might just have a chance…

Chapter 24

Branches snap under thundering hoofbeats and I slow our pace, taking a deep breath of forest air. A large row of pines is situated to the right, and I stop Stardust underneath the closest one.

This should be good…

I wad my zip-up into a ball and carefully wedge it between two lower branches, making sure that the purple's most visible at a distance.

I turn my mare and pat her neck. "Good job, girl. We might just win this." We take a few steps away from the tree, and I scan my surroundings. I wait and wander a few more steps. Patience. Hopefully, Liz and Conner get their flag in time.

An irritating voice echoes from a distance. "Thought you were clever, huh? Splitting up like you did. But now you're left alone and defenseless."

James. Why'd it have to be him?

A shiver runs down my spine. He found me.

I whip my head toward his voice and spot him in the clearing to my left. "You'd like to think that, wouldn't you?" I snap, trying to straighten my shoulders and calm myself.

He closes the distance between us, and I study his intimidating dapple-grey Pegasus. It's limping ever so slightly. It's injured.

He must've pushed him too hard to get here, and he's made himself weak because of it… My eyes flick up to his hardened glare.

"So, where's the flag? We both know you can't defend it against me. Why don't you save yourself the trouble and just hand it over?" He snarls.

Just pretend I have the real thing. Pretend.

I shift my hips and square Stardust to face him, blocking the path to the tree further. "What makes you think I have the flag?" I don't break eye contact.

His laugh is humorless as he grins. "Oh, come on. I'm not falling for that one. Foolish though, that you think you can stop me."

Good…maybe his pride will be his downfall. If he believes I have it, I just have to stall and give them time to get Jame's flag. Just a few more minutes. "You injured your Pegasus. You should probably have him checked out."

I point to its leg.

His eyes flick behind me and lock onto the purple fabric. "Nice try, little legacy."

Crap…

They lunge forward in a split second. I barely have time to shift my hips and turn Stardust and me away from the impact. My heart lurches, and we regain our balance. The buzzer goes off on my wrist. Someone found a flag.

The game is over! I twist my head to look over my shoulder just as James reaches the tree and unravels my decoy zip-up. He whips his head around, his brows coming together as he glares at me. "You little—" he growls.

I squeeze my legs to urge Stardust on, and we burst forward, racing back down the mountain trail. Hoofbeats sound loud behind me. I need only to beat him back. Just beat him back!

When we reach the bottom and take off into the clearing, the other applicants come into view. We push hard to the finish line, our hearts hammering against our ribs, sweat stinging my eyes, and wristband vibrating. Liz crosses the line. So do Gemma and Ashley like flashes of lightning.

Nathaniel comes into view, arms folded as usual across his chest. I squint my eyes and tilt my head to see James closing in behind, Conner and Jessica on his tail.

I turn back and pump my arms, finding a smooth rhythm with her neck as we near the finish line.

Almost! Almost there!

I suck in a breath as we cross it. "Whoa, girl!" I pant and pull back the reins. A smile spreads over my lips. "We did it!"

Half a second later, James whips by us, followed by Jessica and Conner. The last two. They'll disqualify them. I land and spot Nathaniel again; he's already staring back at me for a long moment.

After glancing down at my boots, I look up, smiling at him as the snap of his instructor's voice calls the group to attention. "Well done! You have completed the first trial race."

He pivots to Jessica and Conner. "You both, unfortunately, won't be flying with us any longer. But good luck to you. You are free to go."

I unstrap my thighs and dismount. As the applicants go their separate ways, we offer our goodbyes to Conner and Jessica. I look back toward the stables as Jamie approaches from a distance.

Nathaniel clears his throat next to me, and I'm now completely aware of his new proximity. "I knew you could do it." He rubs the back of his neck. "You did—good." His voice is delicate and calculated as if he might say more.

My eyes lock with Jamie's as she strides closer with raised brows. I let my eyes flick back to his for a moment. "Thank you—I guess it worked out."

Jamie claps my shoulder casually, interrupting our conversation. "Hey! I knew you'd beat those guys! Now we can go dress shopping in the morning."

Subtle Jamie…

I smile over at my friend. "Well, I didn't get first place, but third isn't so bad." I laugh out of pure adrenaline. "I guess we can go shopping now." What is wrong with me? Why am I so nervous?

Nathaniel steps back, stuffing his hands into front pockets. "I'll let you girls—ah—be girls." His gaze falls back on me. "I'll see you at the dance tomorrow."

For a moment, I am lost in deep blue eyes. "Yeah—see you at the dance."

Jamie's eyes flick between us. Heat rushes to my face, and I click to Stardust, leading her towards the stables. This time, Jamie catches up with me. "Hey! Come back here! Tell me everything." She demands.

Chapter 25

Grasping a purple silk dress, I hold it up in the store's aisle. "Jamie, what about this one?"

She scrunches her nose and shakes her head. "You can't do purple; every first-year girl or applicant will want to wear the school colors."

"Fine, but this is taking forever." I lean against the clothing rack and groan. "What color are you thinking of getting?"

Jamie perks up. "I'm going for red!" She holds up a fitted crimson knee-length dress. "This has got to be the one!"

Smiling at her, I sigh. "Jasper's gonna love it. That's perfect for you."

I swipe through another dress rack at the local thrift shop. "Now, I just have to keep searching for mine. You sure I can't just wear sweatpants?" I tease.

She snorts and rolls her eyes. "No, but nice try! I'm

136

gonna go try mine on. Good luck!"

"Thanks," I whisper to her back as she takes off to the fitting room.

The doorbell rings as a couple of girls from the academy roll in. Tess leads the pack, and I turn down the next aisle to avoid being seen by them. I fumble through the clothing rack and pull out a glittering gold strapless dress. Hmm…

I spin, heading towards the fitting room.

Tess rounds the corner, stepping in my way. "That would go perfect with my necklace! I'll take that!" She bursts forward, ripping it from my hands. "Thanks, Rosa. You did all my dirty work!"

What the heck? Who does she think she is? I bunch my hand into a fist, seconds away from snatching it back. Pick and choose your battles, right? That's what grandma would say if she were here.

It's not worth giving her the reaction she wants.

I take a calming breath, uncurling my fingers. "Fine, you can have it."

She laughs. "Like you had a choice…"

Tess turns, striding over to her girl squad and as soon as she reaches them, they all burst into laughter.

Whatever, just ignore them. She can have it. I take another deep breath, striding back down the dress rack.

Blue silk catches my eye and I pause.

The fabric is soft and light as I hold it up in front of me. A floor-length baby blue silk dress with delicate but beautiful straps. "I think…I have a winner." I whisper, draping the fabric over my arm as I head to the fitting room.

* * *

I stand in front of my dresser and slip into the beige heels. "You would never know these shoes were only five dollars!"

Jamie adjusts her red dress straps and strides across the room. "I know, right? We found killer deals today."

I straighten my shoulders and pull down on the light blue fabric that clings to what little curves I possess. "I wish I had more jewelry to go with this. A necklace, maybe?"

Jamie practically sprints over to her dresser. "Oh, I have just the thing." She pulls out two silver dangling earrings.

"Here, you can wear these. Just to borrow though…" She smiles.

I grin and take them from her palm. "Thanks!" She's kind of like having a personal stylist, and it's weirdly fun. Is this what it's like to have a sister?

I shrug. "Now for my hair. Any ideas?"

She taps her fingers on her chin. "Hmm, probably half up."

"Okay, I'll give that a try." I stride over to the small mirror and pull the front of my loose silver strands back with a small clip, leaving the rest to hang over my shoulders.

The matching earrings shimmer against my neck as I slide them in. "Okay, I think I'm ready." I turn on my heel to face my roommate.

She places her hands on her hips, striking a pose. "Me too!"

We stride to the door. "Wait till a certain someone catches sight of you!" She teases.

I scoff. "Don't be ridiculous!" A nervous laugh bubbles out. "Wait till Jasper sees you!"

She links her arm in mine. "But first, let's not kill ourselves in heels going down these darn steps..."

I shake my head, then salute her. "Aye aye, Commander." I love seeing this side of her; maybe she's not as scary as I thought? Well, probably not.

I trip over my dress and catch myself just in time before I

faceplant. Yikes that was close…

She giggles, pulling me up. "Rosa, I gave you one command! Don't fall!"

I blow out a dramatic breath. "Please, I was just testing your reflexes!"

We burst into laughter as we stumble our way down the stairs to begin the night's festivities, butterflies dancing in my stomach as we stride down the hall.

Here goes nothing…

Chapter 26

The dance floor swirls with flickering lights, illuminating the crowded room. Spinning around, my heart pounds in rhythm to the music as Jamie and Jasper take the floor once again. I smile at their blossoming relationship, completely captivated by the way they look at each other. Tess and her clique take over the middle of the room, happy to be the center of attention tonight.

Aidan flails his body around next to me, dancing like a wild animal and panting for air. "Need water! Be–right back!" He blurts out and retreats.

Laughing at my silly friend, I take in this moment. Just being here is a small sliver of something that feels foreign. It feels good. It feels like—fun—a kind of enjoyment that I haven't experienced in what feels like forever.

Since...mom. I wish she were here for this.

I snap out of my thoughts, letting my body relax and flow to the beat until the song changes, slowing it down for the evening. The atmosphere immediately shifts. Couples start frantically searching to unite with each other, and singles look to find a partner.

Whelp…I guess all my fun is over now.

My heels click on the cafeteria floor as I maneuver my way through the already swirling couples. The table with my iced tea sounds very appealing right about now. I glance behind me as the lights dim low, matching the mood to the end of the evening.

Turning back, I bump into someone. My eyes trail up a crisp black suit to be met with deep blue ones. "Hey—sorry about that." Nathaniel clears his throat. "Um, would you like to dance?"

I stand there for a moment, speechless. "S-sure," I smile and glance around. "Is this really all right? Isn't Mr. Flawless scared of ruining his reputation?"

He smiles back and extends his hand. "You're just gonna have to find out."

Hesitantly, I slide my hand into his. His eyes roam around the room before focusing back on me. He looks…nervous?

"Well, that's definitely reassuring." I tease.

He guides me to the edge of the dance floor and pulls me in, leaving a foot of space between us. I extend my hand to his shoulder as he places his warm arm around the curve of my back. The distance between our bodies is interesting, though it's electrifying as we sway to the music. Perhaps he keeps so much space between us in order to keep his good-boy image up for those watching.

Or maybe he isn't actually interested…

"You know, you could win. Find your place here," he says, voice dropping low to my ear.

I do a little spin and step back towards him. "You sound like my grandmother, you sure you don't know her?" I tease. "But speaking of my grandma, I need to talk with Henry. He said he had some news, but that it could wait until after the celebrations. I'm not sure what's going on…."

His brow furrows in concern as he meets my gaze. "I haven't heard him mention anything alarming during our meetings, but maybe he just wanted to let you enjoy the night. You did well in the first race, I'm impressed. You're showing real potential to make the team."

I give him a small smile. "I hope you're right. And thank you."

He spins me again, and for a moment I forget all the narrowing eyes on us. Perhaps I could fit in here. Make my mom proud.

My eyes flick back up to meet his. "I just have to beat everyone and win a competition…" I shrug my shoulders.

"You know, all simple stuff." I let out a breath.

The corner of his mouth turns up, and his eyes soften as he leans closer. "Piece a cake. I bet you can do anything you set your beautiful mind to."

Heat rushes to my cheeks, and I raise a brow. "Did you just call me beautiful?"

Nathaniel smiles, gently shaking his head. "Now, Ms. Lynch, I don't have a clue as to what it is you're talking about." His eyes swirl with mischief.

"Ah—alright. I'm just checking." My smile grows.

He is about to spin me, when Tess taps on my shoulder. Her eyes pierce through me as she smiles. "I'm cutting in. You can go now, Rosa."

Before I have time to answer her, Nathaniel speaks. "No, thank you. I'm dancing with her."

Her nostrils flare and she spins, grumbling under her breath as she leaves the dancefloor. Our eyes meet me again and he smiles. I can't help but giggle.

He spins me and pulls me closer. "Maybe I'm not making it clear enough?"

A smile tugs at my lips. "Hmm, I don't know what you're talking about…"

He smirks as we sway to the music for a long moment

until the song ends. I could get used to this place. I could get used to—him.

Chapter 27

I hurry into the stables after breakfast to find Henry. This man has been almost impossible to locate. Maybe he actually is avoiding me…

This thought only has my feet moving quicker in the barn's aisle. As I pass another Pegasus, its whinny echoes another friendly greeting. The scent of leather reaches my nose as I peek into the tack room. He's nowhere to be seen. Where is this man? I'm going to miss class if this takes much longer.

Spinning around, I stride to the back door and peer out. From afar, Henry slowly becomes clearer. "There you are!" I let out a breath. "I've been looking for you everywhere."

He closes the distance, eyes focusing on me. "I know. I'm sorry, Rosa. My mind has been elsewhere. I've been contemplating some things," he says, his voice unusually discouraged.

I look over my shoulder for a moment and then turn back

to him. "Okay. Well, I have only a couple of minutes until class starts. But I wanted to ask about my Grandma June..."

His face fills with what I can only assume to be dread. "Rosa, I think we'd better go sit down."

My heart sinks into my stomach, blood draining from my face. "W-what? Is she okay..?"

He gestures with his hands to soothe me. "Oh, no. June is still very much alive—I'm sorry to have scared you. But why don't we go sit and I'll explain the rest?"

My eyes lock into his. "The rest?"

He motions his arm back into the stables, and we walk silently to the tack room and sit on folding metal chairs. Henry sighs and rubs his palm over his jaw. "This is not how I imagined this going—"

I sit up straighter. "Okay, now you're really scaring me! What is going on?"

Henry's eyes soften. "Your grandmother's condition has changed. Her health is declining as her dementia has worsened. She is being placed in a home to ensure she has around the clock care. I fear my mother doesn't have much longer," he says, a little above a whisper.

Looking away, I swallow hard. "Being moved? She has a home already..." My eyes frantically meet his steady gaze as the realization of his other words hits me like a blow to my ribs. Wait...

"What did you just say? Your mother?" I demand.

His eyes flit away for a moment before focusing on me once again. "This is not how I wanted you to find out. I had this entire plan and—"

I jump to my feet, cutting off his words. "You can't be serious? That means..."

He raises his palm, attempting to calm the situation. "Rosa, yes. I am your father. Though this is not how I wanted you to find out."

Every interaction that we've had comes crashing down in my mind. His concern for my safety and sense of belonging. His willingness to step in and take care of Grandma—his mom.

Anger bubbles in my chest, and tears sting my eyes. "I can't believe this..."

I take a shaky breath. "You left us. Y-you lied! Mom died, and you weren't even there!"

He stands and rests gentle hands on my shoulders. I must look like a wild animal, but I don't care. Not right now.

My father takes a deep breath, and his eyes soften. "After I realized I had made the biggest mistake of my life, I tried to come back and make it right." His tone pleads with me.

Tears spill uncontrollably down my cheeks. "Really?! How

did you try?" I choke out.

A single tear runs down his cheek. "You don't understand. I came back two weeks later and begged for forgiveness…" He takes a deep breath. "She threw me out and said she never wanted me to be a part of your life."

"So you faked your own death after she was gone? You're unbelievable!" Brushing his hands off, I step away. "You're a coward. I can't do this right now…leave me alone!"

He steps toward me. "Please, Rosa. Let me explain!"

My father's expression softens further, as if composing himself. "We'll talk about this when you're ready."

Even though I see the heartbreak in his eyes, I can't stay and listen to this. I bolt out of the tack room and walk down the aisle to the stables' end. The students are now entering from the other direction as my chest tightens uncontrollably.

I need to get away—I can't breathe. After rounding the corner, pain radiates through my shoulder as I slam into someone. Hard.

A grumble escapes Nathaniel's lips as I pull away. "Ouch. You sure like to run into people a lot…" He mumbles.

I shove past him, barely meeting his worried gaze, and take off towards the treeline. His voice echoes loud behind me. "Rosa!"

I run faster, my lungs already burning. Wind whips at my

tear-stained skin, and I push back a strand of hair. Branches crack, my boots catching on twisted roots as I frantically pump my arms and legs. I don't know where I'm going, and I don't care. I run until my legs give out, then I walk.

When I'm deep in the woods, a sob escapes me, and I stumble to the forest floor. I gasp for air, shoulders shaking as I wrap my arms around myself.

I let every lie, every birthday wish, every secret shred of grief that I have ever felt since my father supposedly passed away, pour out. It all comes to the surface. I'm not afraid anymore, so I let it consume me just this once.

Chapter 28

The sun is about to set through the trees, and I've been walking for what feels like hours. This can't be good. Every fiber of my being feels weighed down, exhausted. I wander over to a fallen tree and sit down. The ringing in my ears subsides, and I rub my temples. "Good move leaving your phone behind, Rosa."

I whisper harshly into nothingness. "Great, now I'm talking to myself." I cross my arms and sigh, staring out into the endless sea of trees. There's gotta be a clue to where I am…I glance up at a tall oak tree. A branch fans out just low enough that I could grab it.

Here goes nothing…

I stride over to the base of the oak and grab the lowest branch, hoisting myself up. The misery of weight training is now paying off. I calm my breathing and reach for the next branch, then the next.

When I reach the top, the branches creak and sway in the

wind. I swallow hard. Just figure out where I am…I tell myself repeatedly. Squinting my eyes, I scan my surroundings in the growing darkness. A reflection catches my attention first in a body of water nearby.

The lake.

I've got to get there and find the pathway back. Branches creak further as I begin my descent, holding my breath when I reach an enormous gap and dangle my legs to step onto it. I make it to the bottom and carefully jump to the ground.

After a long moment, the forest grows quiet. Too quiet as I start forward. That's when I hear the howl, deep and terrifying. I whip my head around, scanning every fallen tree and bush. Nothing. My heart races. I've got to make it back before dark.

Taking off into a run, I head toward the lake. A few minutes later, I approach the beachfront, my breath coming in gasps. My knees give out and I slam into the sand, rolling onto my back. I let out a shallow breath. I made it—kind of.

Rolling over on my elbow, I pant for air. After several minutes, hoofbeats pound through the sand, and I whip my head around. Panic rises in my gut when I see James on his grey mount barreling towards me. Crap…

I scramble to my feet by the time he reaches me. "Whatcha

you doing out here all alone, little legacy?" He circles, his large Pegasus towering over me.

I refuse to cower in his presence, so I force myself to stand tall. "What is it to you? Leave me alone!"

James just smirks, completely unfazed. "Well now, no need to get nasty." He circles closer. "Why don't we just have a nice, friendly chat..."

Everything in me screams to run. "No." I say sharply and on instinct reach for a handful of sand. In seconds I'm hurling it at his face and bolt around them, taking off at full speed down the beach.

I'm so stupid...they'll trample me in seconds.

James shouts behind me, and he mumbles some sort of insult before I hear them closing in. My lungs burn in protest, but I push harder. A large black Pegasus and rider come into view ahead.

Nathaniel?

I risk a glance backwards, and when James spots him riding towards us, he cuts a sharp turn and takes off into the air, deciding it's not worth getting into trouble. I keep running towards them and nearly collide with his Pegasus, gulping for air. "Nathaniel..."

"What on earth were you thinking?" He rapidly dismounts and closes the distance between us. "Where have you been?" His eyes wander over me as if assessing me for any injuries.

My legs feel like jelly, and it takes everything in me not to plop down in the sand in front of him. "I—got—lost."

He steps forward and rests his hands on my arms, his blue eyes never breaking from mine. I can see the internal struggle all over his face.

He sighs. "What happened? Did James have anything to do with this? If he did something to you…" His jaw clenches, nostrils flaring.

Do I tell him that James threatened me? "I—" I choke back a sob. "My father—"

Any composure I currently have shatters, and I burst into tears.

"Hey—hey. Come here." His voice softens as he pulls me into a hug, and I crumble into his arms. He holds me as I cry, and after a few long moments my tears subside, and all I feel is his warm body against mine.

My heart hammers at the further realization of his closeness, and I tilt my head up to meet his gaze. "Th-thank you. I have some news about my grandma. And my father—"

He stiffens. "Is she okay? Wait, your father?"

I shake my head. "Yes, she's doing alright. But she got

placed in a home for around the clock care. But my father…my father is alive. Henry—I mean—Jack. He lied to me all this time."

His brows draw together. "I knew it…I had my suspicions, but it all just made little sense."

I lean back. "You suspected Henry was my father, and you didn't say anything?"

"If I were wrong, well, I just didn't want to ruin anything."

"That's not fair. You shouldn't have kept that from me. I—"

Nathaniel brushes a strand of hair from my eyes, his calloused fingers tracing down my temple. I stiffen. "What are you doing?" I whisper.

He bends low, and his lips brush against mine. For a second I panic then I let my lips press back against his.

Hold up…

I pull away. "You think you can just kiss me and I'll forget that you didn't tell me your suspicions?" I raise my eyebrows.

He tilts his head. "Do I need to try it again?" His lips meet mine, and he pulls away slightly. "Let me know how much it takes—I could keep going."

His grin makes my heart skip, and I sigh into the little

space between us. "Seems like I'm not the only trouble maker around here." I giggle as we break away from each other.

He strokes my hair, circling a strand with his finger. "It was a mistake not to tell you my suspicions. I'm sorry."

His eyes lock into mine once more. "Let's get you back and clean up. Everyone was worried sick, including your father." He retrieves his Pegasus and mounts, reaching out a hand to me.

Hoofbeats rumble in the distance, and I look over my shoulder to see Jamie closing in. She speedily approaches us and slides to a stop mere inches from me. "We've been looking everywhere for you, Rosa! Where have you been?" Frantic, Jamie's voice echoes into the fading light.

My eyes meet hers, and I sigh. "It's okay. I'll fill you in on our way back."

Nathaniel grasps my hand, and I pull myself up to sit behind him. "Come on, let's get back. I don't wanna be out here any longer."

✦

Chapter 29

I stretch out sore limbs on the mat in the gym. My body aches in protest for most of this morning, and I fumble my way through it all. I glance over my shoulder at Tess. She stands with her arms crossed and grumbles impatiently, waiting for the next piece of fitness equipment to open up.

James takes forever next to her, watching his muscled arms flex back and forth. Gemma gets up from the leg press, rolling her eyes, and moves around it to the next phase. Tess smiles, taking the leg press.

Shaking my head, I get to my feet and make my way over to the viewing room, glancing around the gym as I go. Jamie is nowhere in sight. Nathaniel and Henry, or rather, Jack, are sitting and talking behind the glass. They pay no attention to me as I go to the small mini-fridge at the edge of the gym and grab a water bottle.

I take a large gulp, soothing my dry throat. When I turn

157

around, Jack is there. His green eyes focus on me, now reminding me so much of my own. How blind I was not to notice it before?

Everything in me screams it now in his nearness.

My father.

His eyes drift around the gym and back to mine. "Rosamond, do you have a minute to talk?" He asks, voice low.

One heavy look into those green eyes is all it takes for a weight to drop in the pit of my stomach. The eyes of a liar.

I turn away, ignoring his plea, and exit the gym without so much as a glance back. I know I can't avoid him forever, but right now he is the last person I want to talk to. What really matters right now is training. I can't afford to let this crumble me—not now. Not now, after I've come all this way.

***

Jamie snorts and takes another bite of salad. "Yeah, that's what I'm saying. If you want me to ignore him, I totally can." She insists.

I lean forward in my seat. "No, you don't have to do anything. I have issues with my dad, not you. Don't worry about it." I force the most convincing smile I can muster.

She leans closer to Jasper at her side. "Okay, if that's what you really want."

I nod. "Yeah, at least for now."

Jasper puts an arm around her shoulder and whispers something to her. These two lovebirds…

I glance around just in time to see James stick out his foot on the other side of the cafeteria, and Aidan walks right into his trap. I rise from my seat just as his lanky frame trips over Jame's outstretched boot. Aidan's tray of food flies everywhere, showering the floor with spaghetti.

My friend slams hard onto the ground, and I rush over to him in a matter of seconds. "Hey—are you okay?"

Aidan groans and sits up. "Yeah, I think so..."

Laughter breaks out in the room. He panics, dashing from the cafeteria. I turn to James, frustration building in my chest. He can't just get away with this. Not this time.

"What is wrong with you?!" I demand.

James shrugs, giving me a toothy grin. "I don't know what you're talking about, little legacy."

His friends chuckle beside him. Ashley smirks, leaning

closer to James. Apparently, she has chosen a side. This is wrong, and he's going to get away with it.

I narrow my eyes. "I saw what you did. Leave him alone! You—you jerk!" I snap.

He stands and pokes my shoulder. "What are you gonna do about it if I don't?"

His foul breath lingers in the air, and I force myself to stay calm. My eyes lock into his, and I could cut the angry tension between us with a knife.

I straighten my spine in confidence, the cafeteria silent in anticipation. He's always gonna be a bully, isn't he?

I don't realize how strong the urge is to punch him square in the jaw until my fist is flying towards his face. So much for staying calm!

Here goes nothing...

My fist connects with its target, sending jolting pain through my fingers and arm. He recoils, shock plastered across his smug face. I did it! I did it?

The group behind him bursts into laughter as I stride away, shaking out my hand. What did I just do?
I hurry through the tables and leave as fast as I can. Right now, I've gotta get out of here.

Behind me, James calls out. "You're dead meat, legacy!" He's probably realizing what just happened in front of all his friends. I swallow hard and step out the door into the hallway, reality crashing down on me. Crap. What on earth did I just get myself into?

I let out a breath, placing a palm on my forehead. What is wrong with me?

Getting some distance between James and me is probably the safest idea right now, or before I get pulled into some sort of office. I stride down the hall and search around for Adain at the same time until I realize. The stables, he's probably with the Pegasus.

Chapter 30

Man, this kid can run fast. "Aidan, there you are. You okay?"

He rises from a wooden trunk in the aisle of the stable, smoothing down his jeans with the palms of his hands. "I'm okay. It's not the first time he's tried to make a laughingstock out of me."

I dramatically shake out my aching hand. "Well, hopefully he won't be bothering you anymore. But I think I just made the target on my back much, much larger."

He raises his eyebrows. "How so?"

I stretch out my fingers and curl them into a fist. "The jerk got a taste of my pent-up anger, I guess?"

His eyes grow wide. "Whoa, whoa, whoa. You hit him?!"

I shrug it off, though my hand is killing me already. "Yeah. I guess I took some of my family issues out on him too. Though I wish I could've gotten him better." I smile. "Side effects of it being the first face-punching in all."

Aidan seems to light up at my words. "That's so cool! You really did that for me? I wish I could've seen the look on his face!"

I giggle and shake my head. "Sorry, but I think I'm gonna pass on any future fistfights. But—it felt good to wipe that smug look off his face."

He grins, and it reaches his eyes. "Oh, come on! I'd give anything to see that!"

It feels good to see him back to his chipper self. I shove his shoulder. "I miss hanging out. Sorry, I've gotten so busy with everything. Wanna help me groom Stardust?"

He straightens his shoulders. "You bet!"

* * *

I wait my turn in line at the lake. Stardust shifts in the sand, and anticipation fills my stomach like it does every flight practice. After James and Liz land, Ashley and I get ready to race.

We nod to each other, taking off at lightning speed. I've gotten used to the flip in my stomach as we blast off into the powder-blue sky. They take the lead, and I adjust my hips to the sudden shifts and changes to maneuver next to her. I lean down and stroke Stardust's neck as we near the other side of the lake.

Just as we are closing in, I shift my weight, urging my mare down and under to the left. We plummet down, hooking low underneath Ashley and her Pegasus. My stomach drops.

I glance up as shock spreads over her features, but not for long. She whips around, and we both push hard to the finish line. The rhythm of wings flapping matches the pace of my heart. Almost there!

As Ashley closes in, the wings of her Pegasus grow dangerously close. She wouldn't sabotage, right?

I push those thoughts away as my body shifts too far to the right. She's too close! I panic and quickly try to adjust myself. Don't fall. I can't fall. In the moments it takes for me to regain my balance, we approach the finish line.

Ashley places first, grinning widely as she touches down onto the beach. I land and calm my breathing. What was she thinking? She could've injured both of us!

I ignore her burning gaze. The applicants who were playing nice before...aren't playing around now. I've gotta wake up. It is truly every man for themselves, and I was an idiot to think otherwise.

Nathaniel strides in front of the applicants once again. "Because we are down to an uneven number, this changes the training strategy up a touch. Would anyone like to volunteer to race again against Gemma?"

James puffs out his chest. "I'll race again," he says arrogantly.

I watch as they ready themselves and burst into the air. As always, he wastes no time and aggressively takes the lead. After a few minutes, the race ends swiftly, James taking first. Nathaniel moves forward, clearing his throat. "Okay, that concludes today's flight practice. You're dismissed!" He orders.

Gemma straightens. "Last one to dinner is a rotten egg!"

James snorts. "Real mature!"

Gemma and Liz exchange a glance before they barrel down the path at a canter. James and Ashley soon follow, calling after them like lunatics. They're acting like ten-year-olds, but it's kinda funny.

I giggle and look over at Nathaniel just as he's closing the gap between us. "You don't wanna run after them too? Looks fun…" He teases.

I raise my eyebrows and sigh. "There is someone else's company that I'd prefer more than running off like a maniac." I say, testing the waters.

He swivels his head, pretending to search around me. "Who is this lucky person you speak of?" His grin is contagious, and I can't help the growing smile on my lips. I place a finger on my chin. "Hmm. Wouldn't you like to know?"

His eyes soften. "You know, we still haven't talked about what...happened."

Heat builds in my cheeks. "What?"

I know exactly what he is referring to, and my lips tingle as I dismount and face him. Nathaniel steps closer, placing a hand on Stardust's neck. "The kiss. Or should I say—" he coughs. "Kisses."

I cut him off. "Ah, yes! That!" I tease.

He smirks. "I mean, I could remind you...if you're unsure?"

I shove his shoulder, trying to hide how his closeness makes my heart race. "You would like that, wouldn't you?" I mock him.

He raises his hands in the air, palms facing me. "Hey—I'm just saying. Anything I can do to help you remember." His voice is smooth and calm, unlike the instructor's tone I've gotten used to. This side of him is calm and playful. Gentle even.

I lean closer. "Well, what are you waiting for?" I breathe.

His eyes spark to life at my words, and he steps in, reaching his hand out to caress my cheek. "I thought you'd never ask." His lips press against mine, lingering softly.

Every second is exhilarating, but I pull back and let out a breath before smiling. "I may need reminders more often."

His hands cup my face, his expression shifting into concern. "Rosa—I have to help you win—we have to train harder. I can teach you more, but we don't have long before the second race," he says, almost breathless.

He keeps his eyes on me while I remove his hands from my face and lace my fingers in his. "Okay, let's do this." I breathe.

Chapter 31

Nathaniel and I have spent most of the evening in the training dome, practicing landing and taking off exercises. I urge Stardust faster and faster, while shifting my weight at the right time and landing again in the sandy arena.

He waves me back over. "I have an idea...but you're going to have to trust me."

Stardust shifts below me, and I take a deep breath. "What do you have in mind?"

"Since the arena is empty at the moment..." He strides into the viewing room and comes back with a purple bandana. "Here. Put this on as a blindfold."

"Are you out of your mind? I can't fly blind..."

He strides closer, handing me the bandana. "Who said anything about flying?"

A knot twists in my stomach, but I nod. "Alright…" I wrap it around my face, immediately regretting it. "Now what?"

He laughs, his boots shuffling backward. "First, take a deep breath. Second, let go of the reins."

Brushing Stardust's mane, I snort. "You've got to be kidding me…"

"You need to become one, fall in sync with each other. Let your body learn her movements and react on instinct. Muscle memory."

I drop the reins, taking in a large breath and cautiously letting it out. "I'll try."

Resting my hands on my thighs, I urge my mare forward by squeezing my legs.

"There you go!" Nathaniel says.

I shift forward too much, but regain my balance. "Okay, girl. Show me what to do." She walks around the arena, guiding me as I talk to her. It's like unlocking a whole new sense as I listen to her breathing, feeling every heartbeat.

With every stride, I let my hips sway with her, and concentrate on engaging every muscle in my legs and core.

"Now, ask her to turn by only using your hips and your right leg. Apply just enough pressure to get her attention."

I nod, focusing on the task at hand. Shifting my weight and applying pressure with my right leg, I ask her to move out to the left. Stardust turns, understanding my instructions. Yes! This is amazing!

"Nice work!" A voice calls out, but it's not Nathaniel. I rip off the blindfold to see Aidan and my father standing next to him in the arena's corner, beginning to clap. I grasp the reins and urge Stardust over to them.

As I approach, my heart rate spikes when my father smiles at me. I'm not sure I can deal with him right now. Nathaniel gives me a warning look, as if he's just as surprised as I am.

Aidan steps forward. "Do you want me to take Stardust and cool her off for you?"

I unstrap my thighs and dismount. "No, it's okay. I'll do it. Thanks."

Without looking at my father, I lead my mare out of the domed arena and down the pathway to the stables.

Chapter 32

My mother glances back from the front seat of the SUV, a laugh escaping her lips. "You crack me up kid, try that one on your teacher."

I smile, soaking up the last few minutes before she drops me off at school. She shakes her head. "This interview better go well...wish me luck?"

I glance out the car window. "Here goes nothing, right?"

"Here goes nothing, darling."

Time stands still when the truck slams into the driver's side, ear-shattering glass flying everywhere. I bolt straight out of bed, holding my chest and gasping for air. Taking a deep breath, I press my palms to my face, attempting to calm my breathing.

Dream. Just a dream.

After a long moment, I lace up my boots and grab my sweatshirt, heading for the door. By the time I make it to the front gardens, another tear makes its way down my cheek. A figure appears as I approach the small stone bench.

"I was hoping you'd be here." I whisper into the darkness.

Nathaniel scoots over to make room on our bench. "Was wondering when your nightly escapades would start up again…"

Quietly, I sit next to him, a long moment of silence passing before I muster up the courage to speak. "Nightmares—that's why—I need fresh air. It's how I've been able to escape it. Though the stars here are much more distracting than at home."

He scoots closer, resting his arm behind me on the back of the bench. "Nightmares?"

I bring my knees up, wrapping my arms around my legs. "Yeah, the accident that killed my mom. Some days it feels like it was yesterday; other times I feel numb to it, pushing it down. If I can go a week without reliving the worst moment of my life…"

Nathaniel wraps his arm around me, pulling me close. "Well—I'm here now. Maybe I could scare off some of those bad dreams."

Giggling, I shake my head. "You'd do that for me?"

He holds my gaze. "Without a doubt."

I breathe out. "In that case, draw your sword because I have lots of nightmares..."

He tilts his head back, gazing up at the starlight. "When I was twelve, my younger sister Keira almost drowned. We were goofing around when she slipped off the pier—I didn't know she hit her head when she fell and after she didn't come back to the surface, I think my heart stopped beating..."

Leaning closer, I rest my head on his shoulder. "What happened?"

"I panicked and dove in after her...if I had been too much longer, she wouldn't be here. I'm not sure how I would've lived with myself if something awful happened to her I could've prevented."

I swallow hard. "You saved her; that's all that matters..."

He sighs. "Yeah, she's a first-year here at the academy now. You've probably seen her around."

I sit up straighter, the realization setting in. "Wait, I know her! She's friends with Jamie...she's the one who invited me to the cliffs for a camp out that night."

"Ah, yes! Your little cliff climbing shenanigans."

I giggle. "Hey—I scaled the thing like a pro!"

He stands abruptly, holding out his hand to me. "My lady."

I take his hand, playfully shoving him. "You big dork."

His hand grips tighter around mine as he takes off into a run. "Come on!"

What the…? "Where are we going?"

He tugs me along with him. "I'm gonna cheer you up…"

I sprint to keep up with him as we barrel through the pathway in the garden. "Ok–ay!"

Chapter 33

The Pegasus whinny, all now stirring from our abrupt entrance into the stables. We sneak down the dark aisleway and Nathaniel pauses, striding over to his gelding's stall. "Care for a moonlit flight?"

I giggle, catching myself from being too loud. "We're gonna get caught."

He slides the halter over Flame's large black nose. "If we do, they'll have to catch us first…"

I shake my head. "Then what are we waiting for?"

"Grab the girths?"

Moving away from the stall, I quickly grab the girths from the tack room. When I return, he has Flame all ready to go in the center of the aisle.

We both move fast with the girths, carefully tightening them correctly. I grab his arm, pulling him closer and press my lips against his cheek. "Thank you, this is exactly what I needed."

Nathaniel turns, facing me fully. "Anytime." He runs his fingers through my hair at the back of my neck and kisses my forehead. "Anytime."

We walk hand in hand and stride out the back door of the stables. He mounts up first, securing his leg straps, then pulls me up, and I do the same.

He takes a deep breath. "Ready?"

I wrap my arms around his waist. "I'm ready."

My stomach flips when we take off into the sky, and I hold on tightly to him. We soar over mountain after mountain, climbing higher and higher. The stars fan out around us, and I can't help the smile that tugs on my lips. This is exactly where I'm supposed to be right now. I need to make it here. I need to win.

Chapter 34

Today is race day. I walk back to the stables with Jamie after breakfast. The sky rumbles and cracks, sending a shiver down my spine. Jamie whips around to face me. "I'm not so sure you'll be having the second race today…"

I tilt my head, noting the black clouds rolling in over the mountaintops. "They wouldn't make us compete in a storm, would they?" I hope she doesn't pick up on the panic in my voice.

She sighs, raising her dark brows. "Your guess is as good as mine, but for your sake, I hope not."

Blood drains from my face. There is no way I'm flying in a storm like this. They wouldn't make us do that, right?

Jamie must see my horrified state because she shoves my arm. "I was just messing! Of course, they will not let you race in that." She brings her voice down to a whisper and mumbles. "Probably—not."

I shove her arm. "Not helping! I should've known you were just messing with me."

We both laugh as little droplets of rain begin to fall.

Nathaniel jogs over to us, making his way out of the stables and down the gravel pathway. "Hey—good thing I'm catching you now! A severe thunderstorm is rolling in, so they will postpone the race until Monday."

Jamie steps back. "I told her you guys wouldn't make them race today." Her eyes flick between Nathaniel and me.

"Well, see you later, Rosa." She takes off back towards the academy.

My smile follows her abrupt departure, and I give her a lazy wave. "I'll catch up with you later." I breathe.

Her sudden absence settles in, and I'm left alone with the boy who makes my heart beat faster. "Hi–" I say shyly.

Thunder rumbles in the distance as huge raindrops now come pelting down. A shiver crawls up my spine as more dark clouds form. This can't be good.

Nathaniel steps closer. "Hi–"

Lightning strikes, and I flinch. "Hi."

I giggle, and his smile broadens. "Maybe we should get inside?" I ask.

"Yes, I need to go talk with Henry—and the rest of the board—about the storm. But I'll come see you later." He brushes the raindrops building on his forehead. "Oh. Did you chat more with your dad?"

I sigh. "No, not yet." Goosebumps form on my arms, and I shiver. "What's gonna happen—if I don't win?"

His ocean eyes stare into mine. "Rosa, what if you do win? You belong here."

I wipe at the water droplets running down my cheek and glance at the puddles forming at our feet. "What about my father? My grandma? Even if I want to, how can I truly stay here after everything?" I say, a little above a whisper.

His hands find my shoulders. "It'll all work out…I talked to your dad about us, and he's okay with it as long as it doesn't interfere with your training or my responsibilities here. Maybe you could forgive him?"

A knot twists in my stomach, and I turn my head away for a moment before looking up at him. "You use the term dad too loosely. He may be my father but he has never been my dad. Every day I'm here, I have to deal with that!"

Nathaniel steps closer. "I'm sorry—why don't you think about us instead." He wipes at the water pooling under my eyes, no longer from the rain. "Think about Stardust and the life you could have here. The races, traveling, competing, and training…with me."

My heart sinks despite his attempt to smooth things over.

"I think I'm gonna use the free time before the race to go back home and visit my grandma." I close my eyes for a moment before meeting his gaze again.

"You're going to have to talk to him…but I'm sure he'll help you get there and arrange it," he says.

I shake my head, the rain now soaking me to the bone. "You make him sound like a saint…"

He sighs, dropping his hands to his sides. "Maybe he isn't the enemy, and you should just give him a chance?"

"Maybe. Maybe—I should just go." I turn away, frustration building in my chest.

"Rosa, wait. I'm only trying to help." He calls out.

I choke on my words, turning to look behind me. "We'll talk when I get back. I need to see my grandma." He means well, but I can't do this. I can't.

Chapter 35

For whatever reason, the plane ride seemed short. Maybe because a million things swirled through my mind, or maybe it was because I tried not to think about Jack the whole time after he insisted on taking me personally because of the storm.

I step off the staircase of the jet, my dad's presence now looming behind me. I'm scared to go back to the academy…but I think I'm even more scared if I don't.

What would happen if I won? What would it be like to have a dad? Could I really leave my grandmother for that long? The car ride to the nursing home has been quiet. My father is giving me the space I want, but I can tell it's killing him.

He turns the car onto a long, swirling driveway. "Here we are." Jack says, perhaps more to himself than to me. As much as it pains me to see my grandma in this state, what might he be feeling?

I shove those thoughts away immediately. I don't need to wonder; he put me through it already and left me to go through that alone with Mom. I fold my arms across my chest. He doesn't deserve my sympathy, not after everything he put me through.

He parks and looks over his shoulder. "For your grandmother's sake…" He pauses, eyes distant and full of pain. "Please act like you don't want to stab me when I'm not looking."

For her sake only, I'll try. "Will do, just no promises when we leave this place."

He lets out a breath. "Figured as much. Come on."

I get out and walk behind him, the large brick building towering over us. As we approach, the automatic doors slide open, and we make our way to the front desk.

He leans over the counter when a middle-aged woman glances up from her computer. "Can I help you?" She asks.

He smiles at her. "Yes. I am here to see my mother. June Lynch."

She types on her computer. "Alrighty…she is in room seventeen. Just down the hall." She points to the right before gesturing to a paper on the desk. "First, I just need you to sign in on the visitor sheet."

Jack grabs the pen and signs. "No problem. Thanks."

I follow him to the room, and we pause at the closed door. He tilts his head toward me. "No dagger eyes, remember?" He raises an eyebrow.

I uncross my arms. "Yeah..."

He turns to give a small knock before we enter, and I take a deep breath. The room is small, much smaller than I expected. She sits across the room; this time recognition does not spark into her eyes.

She stares at us from her bed in the corner of the room as if we are strangers. She looks different—she looks older.

No words form on my lips as I take her in.

Jack steps forward. "Mom—it's me, Jack. Rosamond and I are here to see you," he says.

There is a long moment of silence before Grandma June speaks. "I–I'm sorry, who?" She mumbles.

Pain explodes in my chest. She doesn't know who we are? She clutches her white nightgown, eyes filling with further confusion.

Jack looks back at me, his eyes full of the same pain that I feel growing within me. I can't do this. "I'll be back—"

Any composure that I have breaks as I hurry into the hall. I knew this day would come. Yet now, it's real. It's happening, and I can't do anything to stop it.

A nurse passes me, wheeling an old man down the hallway.

She stops for a moment and turns back. "You alright, sweetie?" She asks, her tone soft as if I might break.

I nod my head, tears stinging my eyes. "I'll be fine. Thank you."

The nurse gives a small smile. "If you need anything, I'll just be down this hall."

I sit there and listen to muffled voices coming from inside her room. My chest heaves, heavy with pressure. Hot tears spill down my cheeks like a flowing river, soaking my sweatshirt. I hold my breath for a long moment, wishing the pain away, but it doesn't work. Another staff woman passes me, but I don't care. Nothing is going to make this better.

Nothing.

Her mind is gone, and I'm losing the last piece of home I have left. I cup my hand over my mouth to keep quiet. Her bright smile flashes in my mind. I can still see Grandma's mischievous grin and the way she would scheme to get sweets, as if it were yesterday. The way her face would light up when she got her way…

I laugh, choking back a sob. This isn't how it is supposed to happen. I should have been there for her all this time. I shouldn't have gone away. She's supposed to remember who I am; I should've never left her side. Time seems to stand still for a few long moments, and I wipe my eyes with the sleeve of my hoodie. Taking a shaky breath, I force myself back into the small room. I've got to face this; she deserves that—even if she doesn't remember.

Chapter 36

I board the plane after Jack. We didn't say a word to each other on the entire ride back to the airport, though for different reasons than on the drive there.

He pauses and gently rests a hand on my shoulder in the jet's aisle. "I think we should go back and see her before the last race. The doctors don't know how much time she has left." He scratches his jaw, a silent pain hanging between us. "We could fly back into poor weather, so try to stay seated and buckle in."

I nod, though it feels like his words are a million miles away—like I am a million miles away. "Okay." I turn down the aisle and take a seat in a cushioned chair.

He disappears to the front of the plane, and I lean back. My head is now throbbing, and I want nothing more than to sleep. To forget... But who can forget? My grandma is dying, and my father has betrayed me my entire life. The engine roars to life, and I buckle up. I sink back into the seat, closing my eyes. And then there's Nate…he wants me to stay and win. To build a life there, perhaps together. He was only trying to help, and I just stormed off like a jerk. That wasn't fair of me at all.

I press my palms to my face, a grumble escaping my lips. I don't wanna mess anything up with him, not when something amazing is just starting between us.

How could I have been so rude?

Queasiness fills the pit of my stomach. I need to apologize to him and hope he understands. Hopefully, I'm not too late.

* * *

A gentle thud on my dorm-room window pulls me out of a restless sleep, and I shuffle to open it quietly. A guy's figure comes into view.

What on earth?

Nathaniel steps out from under a large tree below, the darkness hiding his expression. Maybe he can't sleep either? I don't blame him, with how I acted.

187

He steps closer to the building. "Come down and meet me in the front garden. Our spot," he says.

A moment of silence hangs between us.

"I'm sorry for how we left things…I was only trying to help."

A lump forms in my throat. "Hold on, I'll be right down. Meet you there." I close the window and glance over at Jamie. She is fast asleep and somehow oblivious to our entire conversation. Either that, or she's pretending to be asleep for my sake.

I fumble through my clothes, grabbing my favorite hoodie and boots. I slip them on and exit the dorm, heading down to the landing. Quieting my steps, I walk down the staircase and out the front doors into the garden where we first met. I follow the lampposts and head for the small stone bench.

My breath catches when I see him sitting there, waiting for me. "You're not the one who should apologize—I completely overreacted. I'm the one who is sorry." I rant on. "You were only trying to help, and I blew up."

His deep eyes lock into mine, and I'm sure I can see the million emotions in them despite the darkness. "Walk with me?" He asks. Nathaniel rises from the bench, and we walk side by side down the garden path. He clears his throat. "So, how'd the visit go?"

I reach for his hand, and his calloused fingers wrap around mine. "My father and I rarely spoke...."

I force myself to take a breath and continue. "My grandma doesn't remember who we are anymore. She didn't even know who I was..." I choke back a sob that surfaces all too fast.

He wraps his arms around me, bringing me closer. "Oh—Rosa—I'm so sorry. Is there anything I can do to help you feel better?"

"Sit with me and watch the stars?" I ask.

He gives me a gentle squeeze. "Sure thing. Let's go to our bench."

Our bench, I like the sound of that. I bury my head in his shoulder and look up at the vast sky, full of twinkling starlight. A couple of things in my life are going well, at least. The best part is that I never expected to find Nathaniel; now I can't picture my life without him in it or this academy. What am I gonna do if I don't win? What will happen if I do?

Chapter 37

I watch the clock and attempt to calm my breathing. The race starts in fifteen minutes. I put Stardust's grooming kit away, anxiously examining the others as I pass. Ashley and James stand together with their Pegasus outside the stable, talking just out of earshot.

Gemma stands in the aisle tightening the girth on her Pegasus. "Hey–Gemma. I need to use the bathroom; can you watch Stardust for me?"

"Just be quick. We'll have the lineup soon."

"Thanks. Be right back!" I hurry to the tack room with the cleanest bathroom.

When I return, Gemma's lined up outside the barn, and Ashley strides out of the stables. She flicks her braid to the side and calls over her shoulder to me. "Good luck…"

Aidan approaches me from behind, and I turn to face him. "Hey–I was wondering if I'd see you before the race."

He smiles. "Yup! I got your bridle—you forgot it."

I press my palm to my forehead. "Thank you! I'm sorry, my mind has been, well, foggy."

His eyes fill with excitement. "You'd better get going and line up! You can win this next one for sure!"

A nervous giggle escapes me. "Thanks, it means a lot."

Aidan strides down the aisle as I unclip the cross ties and slide Stardust's bridle on.

"We can do this, girl." I breathe out.

The line of applicants forms, and I lead Stardust to the back of the group behind Gemma. We all start down the path to the lake, and I peer around. No Jamie. I feel sick to my stomach.

Just pretend it's practice, just like everyday training. It's just practice...

My heart races, and I blow out a breath. I lock eyes with Nathaniel before he calls everyone to attention and tells us to get ready.

A moment later, the flag drops.

My heart is in my throat as we take off into the sand, and I adjust my hips as we climb higher. We whip past Ashley and Gemma while James takes the lead. Something snaps, and I fling my head around. What on earth was that?

We bank hard and make our turn, slipping past Liz. "Come on! We can do this, Stardust!" I urge her forward and duck my head low. My Pegasus' heart races below mine.

I shift my weight, and we dip below Gemma and come out in front.

One at a time…get ahead one at a time.

Before I know it, we are closing in behind James as we approach the beach. He whips his head around, lips curling into a wicked smile. Out of the blue, he slows in front of us and forces me to bank hard to the left. I shift my weight fully, but it's too late.

Crap! This can't be happening!

The sound of paracord snapping fills my ears as my stomach drops, my body plunging towards the water below. I fumble with the leg straps still attached to my thighs as I slam hard into the lake. Cold darkness envelops me as a ringing noise fills my ears.

For a moment, time seems to stand still. I fell…

I kick my legs as hard as I can and break through the surface. What's happening? My gaze lands on the beach, and many arms are motioning for me to swim back. I tread water as best I can and watch Stardust land swiftly; her face turning back to me.

Muffled shouts fill the air between us, though I cannot hear what they are saying through the ringing in my ears. I pull at the leg straps and untangle myself from them. It broke…the girth snapped so easily.

I hold on tightly to the girth and start swimming hard for shore. This makes little sense…it should have held up under my weight and more.

I kick my legs harder, and as soon as I am shallow enough to walk and push through, my eyes roam the crowd before me. Nathaniel stands at the water's edge, his gaze fixed on me.

My boots catch in the sand, and I practically trip before him, but he catches me. "What happened out there?" He whispers.

I shake my head and regain my balance. "I don't know. My girth snapped. It's not supposed to just snap, right?"

"You just couldn't take the heat when it came down to it, huh, Legacy!" James snickers, standing a few feet away.

The group crowds around him now. Clearly, he's letting the win go to his head.

Nathaniel's eyes flick to James before meeting mine again. "Something tells me this wasn't an accident." He lowers his voice. "But until I can prove it, I need you to just go along with me. Okay?"

I let out a breath and hand him the broken girth. "Okay, yeah."

He turns and addresses the group. "You know the drill.

Rosa is now disqualified from the competition. Liz, you were second to last place today. This was your last race, too. Congratulations, James, on winning the second trial race. You are all dismissed!"

Jack emerges from behind the applicants as they mount and head back to the stable. I trudge through the sand towards Stardust.

My father approaches me, his eyes full of shock. "I'm so sorry, sweetie."

"You have no right to call me that!" Grabbing Stardust's mane, I jump as high as I can, swinging my leg over her back. Before I can situate myself, I urge her forward, and we speed down the beach.

I picture myself falling, my new dream crashing down with me. Grandma's face flashes in my mind. Could anything get worse? I'm going to lose it all—no—I already have.

A tear slips down my cheek, the wind stinging my eyes. It's all over now. All I need right now is to fly. Stardust fans out her wings, and we lift into the sky for perhaps the last time.

How am I going to leave her? Will I ever fly again? What about Nathaniel and finding my place here? I adjust my body as we make a wide turn, extra careful to avoid sudden movements without the girth to help hold me in place.

Maybe it all was becoming too good to be true, and I got my hopes up for nothing…

Chapter 38

Stardust nudges closer as I stroke her forehead. "I'm really going to miss you, girl." I force myself to leave her stall and hang the bridle on her door.

Nathaniel strides down the aisle, approaching me. "I'm gonna prove that your fall wasn't an accident."

I look at him, my eyes so swollen with tears. "Thank you for everything. Really, if I hadn't—"

He interjects. "Wait, don't. Not when there is still hope!"

I don't reply. Instead, I throw myself into his arms, inhaling his familiar scent. He startles back, stunned by my abrupt affection, but he doesn't move away. Nathaniel holds me tight, and I don't know how long we stand there. He doesn't let go of me, and that is enough. That's all I need right now.

* * *

Packing my bag goes disturbingly fast, as I gather my life here in a matter of minutes. I throw my duffel over my shoulder and stride to the door, peering back at the space I called my own. Everyone here will forget my existence in a short amount of time, no doubt. James, Tess, and Ashley will probably throw a party to celebrate the legacy leaving.

I look to the opposite side of the room. Jamie. Where has she been? Will I even get to say goodbye?

I turn and close the door. I guess it wasn't supposed to happen. Would I even be able to face her if she were here?

When I make it to the bottom of the staircase, Jamie appears down the hall. "Hey! Rosa, wait!" She rushes over to me. "I thought I missed you…what happened? You fell?!"

Peering around, I drag her to the nearest corner. "I can't prove it…but I think someone sabotaged my girth before the race."

She gasps. "No way!"

I place my hand over her mouth. "Shhh." I let her go and force myself to stay calm. "I am being sent home until further notice. Nate—is going to prove it was sabotage." I sigh. "There isn't much I can do about it right now. I just have to wait it out, I guess."

She places her hands on her hips. "Okay, okay. But it was

probably James, and you know it!"

I bite the inside of my cheek. "I know, I know. Nathaniel told me to wait…someone has to prove it first."

Her eyebrows raise. "Nathaniel? Is that his real name?"

I shove her shoulder. "Stop it! Walk me out?"

She nods. "Of course."

"So, where'd you get off on a whim?" I prod.

"My parents—they pulled some strings for a really cool rock band in Las Vegas; I couldn't resist. I'm sorry, it was all last minute." Her grin fades as she continues. "I know they're probably just sucking up for not spending time with me. But—hey—at least the concert was great."

That's rough. At least I know my mom loved me. "Oh, I'm sorry, Jamie."

She swings her arms while we walk. "Don't be. It's not your fault. You know, I think I might just miss having you around here."

We stride through the main doors. Jack and Aidan sit in the golf cart, waiting for me. I glance over at Jamie. "I hope I'll see you soon."

She hugs me, and I try not to let the shock show on my face as she pulls back. "If Nate cannot sort this out, trust me, I will." She breathes.

"Thanks, Jamie. Really, you've been a good friend. Let's

stay in touch."

Nathaniel bursts through the main doors, and I step back. His eyes pierce into mine. "Goodbye." I mutter.

Reading the mood, Jamie gives a quick nod and heads for the door. "I'll call you. We'll figure this out," she says.

After a moment she's gone, leaving me to face this reality. I've got to say goodbye to him.

Glancing back up, I smile, forcing my eyes not to betray me. He smiles back, sadness clear in his gaze, too. How can I leave? I take a shaky breath, tears slipping down my cheeks as I start towards the golf cart and toss my bag in.

My father's eyes lock with mine. "Are you ready?"

I nod. "I guess so…"

After a moment, we speed forward, and I glance back at Nathaniel as he watches us drive off, feet frozen in place. Willing myself to look away, my eyes catch on the Pegasus statue, and I relive the first moment I saw it when we pulled up to this strange academy. Oh, how my feelings have changed since then. My chest tightens. I might never see this magical place again.

Chapter 39

The house is eerily quiet, with no Hallmark Channel blaring from down the hallway. Being here without Grandma is something I'll never get used to.

My stomach grumbles, and I make my way to the kitchen and start rummaging through cabinets for anything that hasn't expired. I settle with a bag of chips and stride down the hall to the living room.

Jack lies sprawled out on the couch. Surprisingly, he looks very comfortable here, and I don't know how to feel about that. "So, um, should we go get something to eat? All I found was a bag of chips," I hold them up and sigh. "Unless you wanna share the rations?"

That brings a smirk to his lips. "You had me at let's get something to eat—I'm starving."

"Technically, we are not starving. We're just…hungry."

What is wrong with me? I could lighten up on him a little…

He chuckles softly and rises from the couch. "Alright, Miss Smarty-Pants. Let's go."

I can't help but smile a little, but I think better of it and catch myself immediately. "Please don't call me that." I grumble.

He shakes his head, striding to the door. "You know, it won't kill you to smile around me."

Maybe it will. How does he know?

I follow him to leave. "I would like to go see Grandma after we eat, if that's okay?"

Jack motions with his hand toward the doorway. "Sounds like a plan."

I pass by him and lock the door behind us, then follow him to the black sedan. The car ride to the restaurant is awkwardly quiet, as neither of us are in the mood for any more small talk yet.

Chapter 40

As Jack and I stride through the hall of the nursing home, I note how the woman at the front desk is extra polite to us today. This time, I observe her name tag. Jennifer. She seems nice.

My heart-rate spikes as I walk next to my father down the hall. I take a deep breath. How am I going to face her like this?

He pauses outside Grandma June's room door and looks down at me. "This is my last visit before I go back to the academy. But I want to be here as much as I can—you don't have to do this on your own anymore." He breathes.

His lips twitch as if holding back a frown. I swallow hard, holding his gaze. He wants to be there for me? Should I let him? "O-okay."

My father spins around and gently knocks on the door before swinging it open. I force my body into the room first, and I think my heart stops beating. Her face, once lively and full of spark, now seems so distant. I peer back at Jack, his frame now pinned in the doorway.

I turn towards her once more and tell myself not to look away, to keep walking. She's lost weight—a lot.

Grandma's blue eyes meet mine from across the room, and I close the distance. "Grams…" I barely choke out.

Her eyes wash over me, and I pray she knows who I am—that I'm here for her.

I climb up and sit on the bed next to her legs and try my hardest to smile. "Hey, it's Rosa. I'm here..."

She doesn't say a word, only stares at me for a long moment before her eyes grow distant again. My chest aches so badly, I beg tears not to come.

A nurse quietly enters and rests a hand on my shoulder. "She's been mostly unresponsive since last night. I am so sorry; we tried to get ahold of your father this morning, but the calls never went through. But I think it would be helpful for her to hear your voice, to really let her know you're here with her," she says in a soothing tone.

Her kindness makes my stomach churn. She doesn't have much longer, does she?

I nod, a tear falling down my cheek. The nurse exits after letting me know to come get her if anything changes. Jack stands frozen in place, his face paling by the second.

I turn back and take her hand in mine. Not too tight, but not too loose. "Grandma, I love it at the academy. I know how much you wanted me to find my place…I did. Jamie has become a great friend; I think you'd like her. She's all tough on the outside, but she's really a big softie. And I met someone who could be really important—I guess—I'll find that part out. His name is Nathaniel…"

Her gaze slowly meets mine, her eyes still far off, but I keep going. "And I know—I know who my father is.

Though I'm still so angry about everything and—"

For a split second her hand squeezes mine gently and she mumbles something I can't make out.

What? I lean forward. "What, Grandma?"

Her cracked lips part again. "Forgive him," she says, barely a whisper. Her hand loosens around mine and the light fades from her eyes. No…she's slipping away.

She's gone. No, no, no. A crushing weight fills my chest. I can't breathe.

I'm a little girl again, crying for her mom to come back, and now the last piece of home I have left is gone. This can't be happening...

Was she waiting for me so that she could go?

A sob escapes me as I stand, still holding her hand in my own. This is happening too fast. Too fast!

A firm hand grips my shoulder and I let go of her hand, spinning on my heel. Jack came in…when did he come in? I think my body is shaking. His eyes are full to the brim with tears for his mother.

I collapse into my father's arms, and sobs shake me to my core. He holds me tighter, brushing gentle strokes over my hair. We cry together, putting our issues aside just this once.

Tears stain our eyes until the sun goes down as my heart shatters into a million pieces. My last comfort—my home—is gone.

✧
✦

Chapter 41

The days following her death go by in a blur, and I don't even know what to do with myself. Three days of lying in bed, barely eating, and refusing to talk to anyone has left me looking like a zombie.

Jack is about to leave for a quick trip back to the academy again, though he's spent most of the time here on phone calls since, making all the arrangements.

Grief seems to have different effects on us, or perhaps he just wants to shove it all down, to not feel the consuming pain that threatens to take over. It always comes in waves—grief like this does—sometimes it's like a kiddie pool wave or the feeling of a small tide coming in.

Manageable. Predictable.

But other times it's like a tsunami, crushing everything in its wake and leaving absolutely nothing but destruction and pain behind. You're left without a floor to stand on. Without a place to call home with the people you love.

I roll out of bed and stumble to the bathroom. The girl who meets me in the mirror looks a lot like the little girl whom I once knew. The little girl who lost her mom and had to take on enormous responsibilities.

Broken. Surviving.

The little girl who almost drowned in sadness and loneliness. I splash water on my face, attempting to get out of my head and be present. Jack's voice calls out my name from the other room. He's leaving…

I take a deep breath and walk out to find him by the front door. "So, you're going then…" I breathe.

His green eyes are red from exhaustion, perhaps from crying too. My father looks as if he's about to bolt. "It'll just be a quick trip to settle a few matters, but I'll be back to help with everything here by tomorrow night. I'll call if I have to stay longer."

He scratches the back of his neck and continues. "I put gas in your car and restocked a few groceries. You should have what you need in the fridge in the meantime," he says.

I have no words for the stranger who stands before me. Though I can tell it's his subtle way of telling me I need to eat and take care of myself and that he loves me in his own way. "You didn't have to do all that—thank you." I try to manage a smile.

That seems to comfort him, and he smiles back. "No problem. If you need anything, just call." His voice is soft, as if I might just shatter.

I cross my arms over my chest, wrapping my cardigan tighter around my waist. "Okay." I mutter.

"Okay, I'll see you soon." He is out the door in a matter of seconds.

Once again, I am left with my thoughts in the emptiness of a house that no longer feels like home. Maybe it will never feel the same again. I will never be the same.

* * *

Time seems to stand still today, and I spend the day watching the Hallmark Channel. For a few moments, I forget that I'm not on my own in this empty house. I'll catch myself glancing over to look for her reaction to a funny scene that plays on the TV. I force myself to snap back to reality again and again.

I'm alone…she's never coming back. Grandma is not here to beg for sweets or to get lost in a book, not even to leave the television too loud for me to scramble to find the remote. Tears cloud my vision as I pull the blanket tighter around me and lounge back further in Grandma's chair.

My eyes grow heavier as I click the volume up louder, as if by doing so I can somehow have a little piece of her closer to me. It is well past dinner time when I can't stare at the screen any longer and I force myself to the kitchen to rummage for anything that sounds appetizing. The only thing that stands out is an old ramen noodle in the back of the cabinet.

Here goes nothing…

Though the taste is not as good as I remember, it seems to settle my aching stomach. After eating, I stride back into the living room and turn off the TV.

A yawn escapes my lips, and I drag my tired limbs to my bedroom and flop into bed. It feels like yesterday I was just lying here contemplating a strange mystical school. Now, memories from the last few weeks come flooding back. Stardust, Jamie, Nathaniel, Aidan, and my father. Just when I was feeling like I belonged, it was all stripped away. It might be for the best; I probably wasn't gonna make it anyway.

Chapter 42

A loud knock comes from the front door, jolting me awake, and I scramble out of bed. I don't bother looking in the mirror and stumble to the door, yawning and stretching out my stiff limbs.

I quickly attempt to smooth my tousled hair before opening the door an inch and peering through. Black and purple clothing catches my eye before my eyes meet his.

Nathaniel!

I swing the door open wide and leap into his arms. "Whoa, calm down there." He chuckles. "It's good to see you too."

I sigh and release my grip on him, and he sets me back down in the doorway. The realization of what I just did settles in as heat rises to my cheeks.

His expression softens as he takes in my appearance. "I'm so sorry, Rosa. How are you doing? I tried to call a few times."

I must look like a disaster. "I've been better. What are you doing here? Where's my father?" I fumble to smooth down my hair and remember that I've been in the same ratty pajamas for far too long.

"I have some news." He hesitates. "Nothing bad, I promise. Why don't I take you to get something to eat?" He takes in my attire once more, knowing exactly what I need. "Perhaps you want to freshen up, though?"

The smile that he gives melts something in my aching heart, and I drink it all in even though I know he's definitely making fun of my outfit.

I smile back. "What? You don't like it?" I strike a lazy pose. A bit of my energy is coming back, and it feels good. "Alright, I'll go get cleaned up."

Nathaniel shakes his head in amusement, his eyes never leaving mine. "I'll go wait in the car."

"I'll be just a minute." I step back inside and close the door. His surprise visit sparks hope in my heavy heart, and I scramble to get ready. It feels so good to see him.

* * *

The waiter leaves our table after taking our drink order, and I lean in. "Are you finally gonna tell me the news?" I prod.

Nathaniel focuses on me. "Good news is that you get to come back…"

"Really? I can race again—wait—what's the bad news?"

He leans forward, resting his elbows on the diner table. "I could not prove that James was the culprit. He somehow got Ashley to confess to it, claiming that it was her idea to get ahead. They removed her from the competition, but James remains."

I shake my head in disbelief. "She must like him an awful lot to take the hit for him like that. I wonder what's in it for her…"

He shrugs his shoulders. "Well, after talking with your father, we moved up the race to throw off any other plans James and Ashley might've had. The rescheduled race is tomorrow." He breathes.

A weight drops into my stomach. "Did you just say tomorrow?!"

The waiter brings our water, momentarily cutting off our conversation. We quickly order our meals, and when he turns his back, Nathaniel is the first to speak.

"Yeah, not exactly ideal for traveling and racing the next

day, but if that means less destruction from James, then so be it. Gemma will race along with you two."

I sink back into the leather booth. "Race them tomorrow? How can I? We should have my grandmother's funeral soon. She deserves that."

"Your father made all the arrangements for after the race. I'm so sorry this is all happening like this—I know it's not what you thought it would be. But you can do anything you set your mind to. I've seen it."

My heart thunders. "I'm not as strong as you make me out to be—"

His lips curl into a small smile. "You're right; you are much stronger than that."

Nathaniel hastily fills the silence. "We'll leave as soon as we can go back and grab your things. I wouldn't contact Jamie to fill her in yet. The less of a heads-up James has of your arrival, the better."

What do I have to lose? Grandma would tell me to go. She'd want me to try my best, right?

"O-okay, yeah. I'll race."

Chapter 43

It's well past midnight when I swing the door open to my old academy dorm room. Jamie bursts out of bed, smiling from ear to ear. "Rosa?! You're back? What happened?" Her voice cracks.

I close the door behind me and switch on the small lamp. "Sorry, I had to keep it a secret. They didn't want James somehow getting a heads-up." I set my bags down. "We are racing tomorrow…"

Her jaw drops, eyebrows coming together. "What? That doesn't really leave you much time to practice…"

A knot twists in my stomach, and I sigh. "Thanks for the reminder!"

She strides across the room, sweeping me into a hug. "I'm so sorry about your grandma, Rosa. I tried to call you, but—"

I squeeze her tightly. "It's okay. I was kind of ignoring my phone for a while; I should have responded. I'm so sorry."

Jamie steps away, brushing back raven hair. "No, it's okay. You did what you needed to do. Don't be sorry. Is there anything I can do to help?"

"Help me win tomorrow?" I ask optimistically.

We both chuckle, and her smile deepens. "I can't promise anything, but I'll do what I can to monitor Stardust before the race. I'll try to keep Tweedle Dee and Tweedle Dumm away from her!"

"Sounds good to me," I agree.

With a deep yawn, she stretches her arms. "Now, let's hit the hay. I'm exhausted,"she says.

"Same." I flick off the light. "Goodnight, Jamie."

Chapter 44

No water? Bile rises in my throat as we reach an enormous field a couple of miles from the academy. I swallow hard. There's no breaking a fall now...

A cool breeze brushes past me, and Stardust whinnies as I steer her to stand in place between James and Gemma at the starting line. Almost every student is here to watch the last race. They must have canceled classes because of this. I feel the intensity of James's unwavering stare beside me, as though his eyes are piercing daggers right through me.

I force myself not to look at him again and glance back at Jamie in the crowd. She smiles and gives me a thumbs-up. I spot Tess standing behind her, arms crossed as she rolls her eyes.

I turn my attention from them as Nathaniel whistles, catching everyone's focus. "Welcome to the last race of the scholarship contest! Thank you all for coming!"

He shifts a dark backpack in his hands and continues.

"Each applicant will have an emergency parachute pack on their person." He steps forward and hands each of us a slim and seemingly weightless parachute pack.

We all slip them on and fasten the clasps over our chests as Nathaniel goes on. "You will fly across this field and up to the mountain. On the mountaintop, a challenge awaits you. When the challenge is complete, you will all race back down the mountain and over the field to this finish line."

To my right, Gemma shifts uncomfortably beside me. "What will this challenge be?" She asks.

He steps closer to us. "I cannot spoil the nature of the hidden challenge, but Henry will be there to instruct you on what to do." He intently gazes at the three of us. "There will be no cheating, sabotage, or slander. Do I make myself clear?!"

All three of us nod in unison. While I trust Gemma more than James, I can't let my guard down, no matter what. I fidget with my long braid over my shoulder as Nathaniel steps back from the group. "A full-ride scholarship awaits one of you! Applicants, are you ready?!"

The students erupt in shouts behind us. Between the voices echoing and ringing in my ears, it's almost impossible to hear clearly. Gemma stands on the block, mounting her Pegasus.

I take a deep breath, grab Stardust's mane and mount up. My shaky hands fumble with the leg straps, and I close my eyes for a second, forcing another deep breath.

After a few moments, we are all strapped in and ready to go. Nathaniel raises his arm in the air, palm facing the sky, ready to drop. The crowd behind us falls silent for a long moment. I place my hand on Stardust's neck, anticipation filling us both. She knows what to do. We can do this. Nathaniel's eyes lock with mine, and it's clear he believes I can do this. Here goes nothing—no—everything.

He drops his hand.

My heart is in my throat as I brace my muscles and blast off into the field. We gain speed and lift off into the air first. James closes in behind me along with Gemma. Wind whips at my face, and I squint my eyes to see further. "Come on, Stardust! We can do this!"

I stroke her neck and urge her faster. James gets around us and takes the lead. We quickly arrive at the mountain's base, and I lean forward, urging Stardust to climb higher.

My heart pounds as we nearly graze the treetops. Gemma closes in next to us. Come on. Come on. Where is the clearing to land?

We race higher and higher over the mountain. James spots it first. A figure appears in a small clearing, and I adjust my balance, preparing to land. We all barrel down to the open grass. James lands first, and I do second after him. Gemma touches down a moment after me. That was close…too close.

I catch my breath and try to calm my racing heart as I steer Stardust over with the other applicants. As we approach Jack, he talks into a walkie-talkie. Behind him stand three massive hoops. What on earth are those for?

My father clears his throat. "Behold the ultimate challenge! Today will be a test of true bravery. This obstacle will determine who is courageous enough to be on the team."

I swallow hard and glance at Gemma beside me. Her face pales, and I force myself to look away. I need to be brave, right? Am I courageous enough? I fidget with Stardust's mane, pushing those thoughts away.

James straightens on the other side of us. "Nothing scares me. Bring it on!"

Jack smirks. He must think that whatever he has planned will wipe the smug look off James's face. That both terrifies and excites me at the same time as I focus past him, taking in the three large rings.

He steps forward. "Now, you will start when I give the signal. Each of you has a hoop to fly through. From there, you will continue racing back to the finish line on the field. I will go and get the rings ready."

That doesn't seem too bad. Wait, get the rings ready? Aren't they already set up?

I hold in my questions and quickly check my leg straps to make sure they are secure. When I look up, Jack is walking to the first ring and when he approaches it, he lights it on fire.

My heart races as I watch him walk down the line, my eyes glued to him. Each circle ignites into dancing flames. We have to fly through fire...?

I glance at James, the smug look he was wearing now gone, replaced with shock. This might just take all the bravery I have left...

✧
✧

Chapter 45

My father raises his arm high in the air for a long moment. Anticipation builds with every sharp breath. Stardust shifts below me, and I pull her back. "Steady girl, steady. Not yet."

Jack lowers his arm. "Go!"

James hesitates for a moment, and I tear off across the grass. We barrel towards the closest ring, bursting full of flames. This is all I need—a few seconds' head start.

I urge Stardust on, heat radiating from the hoop as we approach. I suck in a breath and lean forward as we leap into the air. Stardust folds her wings against her side, closing me in. My stomach flips. We are weightless.

Before I know it, we are flying through the ring. Searing heat envelops us for mere seconds. Her hooves hit the ground hard. I shift my weight, and we run as fast as we can, taking off back into the air. "Come on, girl!"

I glance behind me, and we make a hard turn back to the

field. James is closing in behind Gemma. I have only a slight advantage…

I can't look back now; I've gotta stay focused. We soar back down the mountain and level out above the field. James closes in on my side. Pure adrenaline courses through my veins. "It's now or never!" I call out to Stardust, urging her to go faster.

The finish line comes into view and something shifts in her when the crowd cheers us on. The students are going wild. We push harder and faster than we've ever flown.

Twenty seconds.

I risk a quick glance at James; panic crosses his face.

Ten seconds.

The crowd of students part, making way for us to land. I need to do this for my mother. Grams. For me.

Five seconds.

I urge Stardust one last time and push to the finish line.

One second…

Stardust's nose crosses the line first. Gemma crosses after James, finishing last. I slow Stardust, making a wide turn. W-we won the race…we won! I laugh in surprise as my mare whinnies.

Wild cheers erupt as James and I touch down in the clearing of students. I gasp for air, and when Nathaniel quickly strides over to me, I smile wide.

He gazes deep into my eyes. "You did it! I'm so proud of you!"

"Thanks!" My place is here now. This is what she would've wanted. I glance up at the clouds and let out a squeal. "I did it!" Tears threaten to fall. For you, Grams. I hope you're proud. Reaching down, I stroke Stardust's neck. "We did it, girl!"

Jamie runs over as I dismount. Her hands shake my shoulders. "Ah! Congrats!" Her smile deepens. "I knew you could do it…probably." She adds.

I match her grin. "Thanks, Jamie! I can't believe it! I guess you're stuck with me as a roommate…"

"I think I can live with that!" She breathes.

Nathaniel clears his throat. Jamie turns. "Hi Nate, sorry, I didn't see you there."

"That's alright." He mutters.

James storms off, making a scene and carrying on. The crowd of students closes in around us, and Nathaniel quickly takes a step, leaning close to my ear. "Meet me at the lake with Stardust after dinner." He whispers, eyes burning into mine for a long moment.

I smile and nod. "Mmhmm."

Jamie laughs. "I just can't with you guys! I'm going to find

Jasper."

As I am about to scold Jamie, two guys burst into our bubble and hoist me up on their shoulders, chanting about the race. The students chime in again, shouting and celebrating as they parade me around.

Aidan takes Stardust's reins from Nathaniel, then gives me a friendly wave. I wave back, heart soaring. This is where I belong…

***

My father finds me with Jamie and Aidan after lunch in the cafeteria. I can tell he's trying to hold it together in front of my friends.

He presses his lips together. "Join me for a walk?"

I turn to my friends and smile. "I'll see you guys later, okay?"

They nod, watching me go. I follow Jack to the front of the academy and out into the gardens.

His steps falter, and I notice the shift in his mood as he looks down at me. "Do you think you could ever forgive me? I'm so sorry—for everything." He sighs. "I know you want space…"

I break eye contact and take a deep breath. "I—" Grandma's words hit me hard in the gut, and I replay her words. Forgive him…

Our every interaction circles in my brain. He really did try to help us, despite everything that happened. He brought me here, sharing a special part of his life. Now I can't imagine leaving here again. I can't stay angry and bitter at him forever; I need to forgive him.

For both of us. For me… "I–I forgive you."

A single tear escapes down his cheek. "I'll do whatever it takes to make up for lost time." He lets out a heavy breath.

"I promise to be there for you until my last breath…like a father should."

Maybe he truly means it?

A huge weight lifts off my chest and I breathe deeply. I never realized how heavy unforgiveness is, and now that it's gone, how light I feel. Perhaps I'll get to know what it's like to have a dad…

"Thank you," I smile. "But don't expect me to call you dad or anything. At least not yet." I tease.

He nods. "Fair, I understand."

My father wraps his arm around my shoulders, and we

continue walking down the pathway. It feels foreign, but I don't shove him away. I won't risk doing that now. For a moment, I'm the little girl who only dreamt of walking alongside her dad like this. Now that day has finally come, somehow filling the ache in my chest.

Jack gives my shoulders a small squeeze. "Your mom would've been so proud of you! You know that, right?" His voice cracks. "My mother, too."

I nod my head and hold back tears that are too close to falling. "I miss them…so much." I whisper.

He smiles, though tears cloud his green eyes as well. "Me too, kiddo. Me too."

Chapter 46

Scanning the shoreline, I stroke Stardust's soft neck. "Hold on, girl. I'm sure he'll be here soon."

I glance around once more for Nathaniel. A cool breeze sweeps across the lake, sending my loose hair into disarray. She stomps her hoof in the sand below me.

A couple of minutes pass, and he emerges from the path, riding his dark Pegasus. By the time he reaches us, a contagious smile spreads over his lips, causing me to grin wider than when I first spotted him. He dismounts a few feet away, and I do the same.

Heat rises to my cheeks as he strides over and lifts me into his arms, swinging me around in a small circle. "How are you doing?" He asks, resting his forehead on mine.

My heart races. "I can't believe this is all really happening."

I lower my voice and sigh. "We are going to hold a service for my grandma tomorrow—I wish she—"

He sighs softly, holding me tighter. "I know, I'm sorry. She'd be so proud of you, just like so many of us here."

Nathaniel places me down in the sand, and I wrap my arms around his waist. "Yeah, my father said that too."

He tilts his head down, meeting my gaze. "So, you've talked to him?"

Nodding, I let out a breath. "Yeah. We talked, and I forgave him. There's still so much; I don't really know how..."

He nods in understanding. "It's okay, it'll come in time. I'm sure he's just as scared as you are."

"Yeah," I smile. "I've been meaning to thank you, if it weren't for you, I wouldn't have flown in the last race."

His expression softens further, and his stare intensifies. "It was foul play...I had to prove it. I couldn't just let James win, and the thought of you not being here, well." He shakes his head, and his eyes dart away for a second before meeting mine again.

My heart skips as I trace my fingers down his jaw. "What about my not being here?" I tease.

He leans closer. "I've always had this place...I love the sky and flying through starlight." He sighs and continues. "Everything about this place is my home. I never thought I could care about someone more than all this. I think I'm—"

For a moment I forget everything around us. Was he just going to say that he...? I smile. "I care about you too."

His grin makes my heart skip before he gently presses his lips to mine and pulls back. "I love you more than I love the sky, Rosa. It feels like home just might be wherever you decide to be..."

"I feel the same way—I love you too, Nathaniel."

He lifts me again, spinning me around. A giggle escapes me. "Wanna fly? I bet I can beat you!"

He laughs. "Someone's feeling a little confident after the big win, huh?"

I shrug my shoulders. "We'll just have to see about that!"

He helps me mount Stardust, and I adjust my leg straps while he mounts too. Our eyes lock once more.

He smirks. "Ready?"

"Oh, I'm ready!"

We speed across the sand and ascend into the infinite sky. This is truly where I belong—this is my new dream.

My home.

ACKNOWLEDGEMENTS

First and foremost, thank you, Heavenly Father, for your Son's finished work on the cross. For dying to take my place and giving me abundant life. Thank you God, for blessing my life with Your unconditional love.

During the hardest calendar year of my life, I wrote this book. Even in my grief, with two angel babies and a failed adoption, God used what was meant for evil and turned it for good.

I feel incredibly thankful for each individual who has encouraged me in my journey as a writer. Thank you to *Amy White* at *The White Editorial* for championing my story and helping me in my publishing journey, I would not be where I am in my author career without her!

Thank you to my *sisters* and *closest friends* for your undying belief in me! I have the best cheerleaders in the entire world, and your feedback has helped me more than you know.

HANNAH FLUKER was born-and-raised in New York. She is a
multi-passionate person who loves horses, Jesus, being a mother, and
gardener. When she's not writing, you can find her tending to her
garden, reading, baking sourdough, or spending time with family. She
lives with her full time missionary husband and one little blessing.

You can follow along with her passionate life on:
TikTok @hannahflukerauthor
Instagram @hanslifegarden_

Thank you for reading Equus Flight Academy!
If you enjoyed this story, she'd love it if you left a review
wherever you like to review books.

www.ingramcontent.com/pod-product-compliance
Lightning Source LLC
Chambersburg PA
CBHW021807130726
47987CB00010B/3055